ALSO BY THIS AUTHOR:

Prim Improper

Improper Order

Pr IMPERFECT

Deirdre Sullivan

Little Island

To my fantastic brother, Tadhg. Let's keep going places.

PRIMPERFECT
Published 2014
by Little Island
7 Kenilworth Park
Dublin 6W
Ireland

www.littleisland.ie

ISBN 978-1-908195-90-6

Design by Fidelma Slattery @ Someday.ie

Typeset in Baskerville. Cover typefaces: Denne Milk Tea by Denise Bentulan and Agent C by Carl Leisegang, also used throughout the interior along with Denne Freakshow by Denise Bentulan, Cute Cartoon by Galdino Otten, Never Grow Up by Kimberly Geswein and Starlight by Des Gomez.

Printed in Poland by Drukarnia Skleniarz

Little Island receives financial assistance from the Arts Council / An Chomhairle Ealaíon and the Arts Council of Northern Ireland.

Supported by The National Lottery® through the Arts Council of Northern Ireland

10 9 8 7 6 5 4 3 2 1

NOTE TO THE READER: IN THE EVENT OF MY UNTIMELY DEATH, PLEASE BURN THIS UNREAD.

But on the off-chance that I'm not dead and instead am letting you read this for some unlikely reason (to clear me of a murder charge or provide me with a convincing alibi perhaps), here are some things you need to know before you start.

In first year, we had this dictionary notebook and I liked it a lot. I love new words, like 'pneumatic' and 'troglodyte'. I added to it almost every day and kept going on with it long after it stopped being homework. I was going to say long after it had stopped being cool but it was never cool. We have that in common, the note-book and I. People are a lot harder to define than words like these:

COSMOPOLITAN: (This has a few meanings.)

Firstly it is a cocktail that women drink in fancy films about shoe-shopping and conditional friendship. It is pink in colour and comes in a martini glass. I once had a sip of one and it was only OK.

Secondly it is a magazine that teaches ladies how to have proper sex. The kind that involves pleasing your man and sucking in your tummy. It also features true-life stories about a range of issues, but people mostly buy it for the **HOT SEX-TIPS**. I have never had any temperature of sex, so I can't vouch for its accuracy. I still like reading it, though, in case I ever want to have a sex Olympics. The more you know, right?

And _thirdly_ it is an adjective that describes someone who is well travelled and urbane and speaks several languages.

ALMANAC: A book old dudes often have in their possession. Content usually involves tidal information and astronomic data and dates that things happen on. But not interesting things like rock concerts or explosions. Geographical things. Not that the stars are boring or anything. I love looking at them and hearing legends about how they came to be and what-not. There are no legends in almanacs, though. Just statistics. They're a bit dry and could do with a few interesting features and improbable sex-tips. Or at the very least a problem page.

My life is full of nouns that need explaining. I wish I had more time so I could do it. I wish I cared enough to try. Is this what growing older means, not being bothered to do things that you kind of want to do but not as much? I would like a dictionary of me and I could look it up and it would just say

Stop
obsessing
Prim.

Everything
will
be
OK.

Just
breathe.

PRIMROSE LEARY: I'm a girl, with hair and a face and things. I don't know if I'm like other people because I've never lived inside of anyone but me. From what I know of them, though, I'm a good deal stranger. I don't imagine other people have rats and therapists and imaginary Viking boyfriends. They must get really lonely.

reaking into a cemetery at midnight is not the finest way to turn sixteen. But midnight was when the night-watchman's shift changed and it was really important to get it done tonight. Roderick couldn't lie in state in his part-time tomb much longer. Dad needed the third drawer of the freezer for other, less ratty things. Like steak.

Roderick was dead, you see. He'd died the week before and because he was such a fine and swishy gentleman, I had decided that the only place for him was my mother's grave. Mum loved Roderick too. We got him the year before she died, when he was young and full of ratty promise.

Roderick had lived up to all his ratty promise. He had been my small best friend for many years and I don't think I would have coped half as well with life and love and loss and loneliness if I hadn't had my rat-man by my side. I had been keeping him in the freezer, wrapped in a piece of purple satin, since the night he passed away. He got rat-cancer. We took him to the vet and Dad said he would pay whatever it took to cure him. But by the time rats show you that there's something wrong, it's usually too late. He'd been tired recently, but I'd thought it was old age finally catching up with his elegant self.

Quote from Prim's mum's diary

≡ 1 ≡

Every night that week, I let him sleep in the bed with me, cosy and huddled, even though it meant I had to change the sheets every evening because, although he was still the most dapper of rats, he was no longer the most continent. Not that it mattered. Continence is over-rated, in my opinion. In the end, I woke up one morning and his body was still there, but he was gone. All stiff and pointy, his mouth agape, curled open in a way it rarely did in life.

We discussed putting him in a little grave in the garden, Dad and me, but in the end there's really only one place he belonged. Dad normally doesn't know about my schemes, but he knows about this one. Enough to turn a blind eye to it at least.

'I am turning a blind eye to this, Primrose,' he said, with the air of a martyr who has been up all week comforting a daughter made of sobs and no longer cares how she gets closure.

'Appreciate it, Dad.'

'No.'

'What?'

'You're supposed to say, "Turning a blind eye to what?"'

'Oh. All right, Dad. Turning a blind eye to what?'

'To nothing, I hope.'

He nodded in that way he thinks is wise. Then we exchanged significant looks, before he dropped myself, Ciara, Ella and Kevin off at the cemetery with a bag full of shovels. Syzmon and Caleb were meeting us there, with the bolt-cutters. We weren't planning on breaking in properly, you understand. But Caleb thought we might bring the bolt-cutters anyway 'just in case'. Caleb loves his bolt-cutters. He had volunteered to come along, even though he doesn't hang out with us half as much any more now that Ella has broken up with him. He is trying to win her back, I think. Also, he is pretty good at this sort of thing, because he has a brother, Seth, who used to do a bit of burglary back in the day. It was pretty easy to break into the cemetery.

Ciara had sewn a little smoking jacket for Roderick, so we put that on him and lit some candles all around Mum's grave. Then we dug a deep little hole (though not too deep in case we hit her coffin) and I placed him gently in. I was bawling at this stage. The others were pretty worried someone was going to come and arrest us for noise pollution, putting pets in people's graves and also trespassing. The big three, like.

I wished Joel were there with me, but we still aren't speaking. I asked Ciara if he knew that Roderick was dead and she said he did, she'd told him all about it. I can't believe he didn't contact me when he heard that. I know he's still mad at me but he was close to Roderick. He should have come to pay his respects even though he's shunning me like I have a highly infectious strain of BO.

I miss Joel. And Roderick. And Mum. Especially Mum, but I've kind of got used to missing her. Missing Roderick is new. And the small rat-shaped hole in my life will not be easy to fill. Once we were finished, we all held hands around the grave and shared our favourite memories of Roderick.

'I liked dressing you up in ridiculous outfits as though you were a doll and not a rat.'

'I liked the way you were always stealing things and hiding in other things.'

'Even when you weed on me, I didn't really mind.'

'I never met you, but I really liked hearing stories about you. Like how you gate-crashed Prim's dad's dinner party that time and made everyone think his home was infested with rats.'

'That was awesome.'

'It really was.'

'I used to think rats were disgusting until I met you. Now I think rats are lovely. Rest in peace, small Roderick.'

'You were my small, greedy, ingenious best friend and I will miss everything about you. Especially your clever little face. Mind him well, Mum, he's great company.'

And I was off again. Ciara held my hand. She's great at comforting people.

Ciara is probably the closest friend I have, now that Joel has turned against me. She has been going out with Syzmon since she was in first year, and they had their third anniversary earlier this year. She is sixteen as well, but a little bit older than me, even though I'm taller. We share a therapist, Caroline, who is better than the one I used to go to after Mum just died, Triona, but not as good as not having to go to a therapist at all.

Caleb had brought a few cans of cider but didn't feel right about drinking them in a cemetery (he's quite respectful like that) so we climbed back over the low bit of the wall and piled onto a bench. Caleb opened the cans and passed one each to Ciara, Syzmon and Kevin.

Ella and I don't drink. Well, I do sometimes, but not on important days. Or anywhere near a car.

Ella doesn't drink because she is on medication that reacts badly with it. Ella has autism and can sometimes get really anxious and weird. In primary school she used to repeat things and get up and turn in circles and sometimes yell at people. Or throw things across the room. She does that still sometimes, at home. So do I, because sometimes your emotions need dramatic emphasis or to pop out more or something.

Ella was pretty angry with me for not putting Roderick down once he got very sick, but my heart was breaking and I couldn't bear for the end of such a lovely ratty life to be my decision and not up to the fates. I was kind of hoping that the fates would intervene. Life isn't like that, though. The fates, or gods, or whatever things there are, are not benevolent. It isn't that they're malevolent or anything, it's just they don't really care about petty little nonsense like our happiness and lives. They've bigger fish.

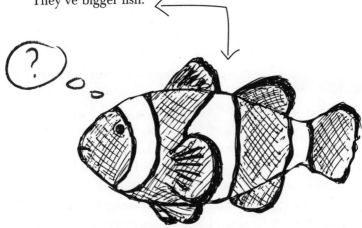

I put my head on Ella's shoulder and smelled the soft leather of her brother Felix's jacket, which she has taken to borrowing against his will. It looks cute on her, kind of too-big in a way that makes her look really feminine and alt-cool.

'Stop smelling me. I am not Felix.'

'Stop being such a grumpus, Ella. I know perfectly well who you are.'

Ella is extremely perceptive and does not mince her words. She also knows that I fancy her brother. Have done for ages. He's kind of the love of my life so far. Ours is a very one-sided love, though, and he rarely acknowledges I exist, except for sometimes when he wants a cup of tea or has things to say and doesn't care to whom and I'm around. I love sometimes. I wish it could be sometimes most of the time. Instead, it hardly ever is at all.

Ciara snuggled down on Ella's other side. Any talk of fancying and she is immediately there. She loves boys and boy-related adventures. This is even though she has only ever had one boyfriend – Syzmon. The two of them will probably get married and Ella and I will be her bridesmaids. I quite like the idea of being Ciara's bridesmaid. She is, as well as being a monogamous gossip-monger, a capable seamstress and milliner. I didn't properly know her when we were in primary school because of how we had different groups of friends and how she used to eat her own hair and be very, very quiet most of the time. We were in the same class. I used to eat my own lunch and be very, very loud most of the time. Mostly with Joel. I miss Joel so much.

'So. You want to smell Felix, eh?' Ciara waggled her eyebrows in an unladylike manner.

I nodded sadly. 'I do. I do indeed.'

Sniffffff

There was no point in trying to hide it. Ella was there and she does not see the point in lies and almost always refuses to keep secrets. She knows I want to smell her brother's jacket, because it has been going on for almost four years now and my nostrils remain aquiver.

'What aftershave does he use?' Ciara is very interested in what brand of smell people have. She can identify specific ones by sniff. It is an almost-superpower.

'I don't know. It smells of – boy?'

Ciara, who had been hoping for something more specific, looked a bit put out. 'Syzmon smells of Hugo Boss. I got it for him last Christmas.'

Then she made the two of us smell Syzmon. And then the other two boys for comparison. Ciara is tiny, so I think the cider might have taken effect at this stage. Although maybe not. She has done stuff like this while sober. Kevin smelled the nicest, Ella and I agreed. Then I was all worried that I should have lied about it because:

A

Ciara got a little bit offended that we weren't sniff-perving all over her boyfriend.

B

I have a long and messy history of kissing and not-kissing Kevin. We are in one of our not-kissing periods. I do not want to be kissing him again. Even though he smells the best out of him, Syzmon and Caleb, I do not want him to think that there is going to be any kissing happening between him and me. We are just friends now. And friends are honest with each other about stuff like how they smell.

I am going to stay away from Fintan from now on. He isn't good for me.

Dad gave me Mum's diaries last night. He's been holding them since she died when I was twelve. They are full of interesting information. For example, did you know that an LP is an album and a smather is a smack? Three and a bit years I've waited for those diaries and now they're here and I don't know what to do with them. Because if I read them all in one big greedy glut, like I do with books normally, her story will be over and I'll have no more of her. I want to be the kind of girl who doles them out sparingly, like a page a day until I'm twenty-one. Not that there's that many. Twelve fat notebooks: three black, two brown, one blue, one red, one pink, one gold, one chequered and two that have fancy marbled covers. I've looked through them and put them in order. Red is first: she was still in school when the books she used were red. I wonder if I should read them in order or skip right to the Mommy – Daddy drama of my birth? A bit of me says that Mum wouldn't like me reading private things. Another bit is too nosy to care.

Quote from Prim's mum's diary

Dad was kind of loath to give them to me. All talk about the past being in the past and so on. I have the distinct feeling he will not come off too well in these diaries.

Ciara asked me about them last night as we were walking to the bus.

'I don't know if I'd want to read my mother's diaries,' she said, looking worried. (She's right to be. Ciara's mum is kind of a wagon who tried to con her out of her inheritance from Grandma Lily. It was this whole big dramatic thing that happened early last year.) 'I don't know if I'd like what I'd read there.'

'I'm sure it'd be grand. You know she loves you. Deep down anyway.'

I linked her arm with mine because it is nigh impossible to hug while speed-walking.

Ciara sighed. 'Very deep down. She keeps bringing up how ungrateful I am. Even when I'm doing something like emptying the dishwasher or putting out a wash, she still calls me ungrateful because I amn't doing it quick enough for her liking.'

'It will be worth it, though. And when you're a famous milliner like Phillip Treacy she will eat her horrid words.'

'I hope so, Prim. I really, really hope so.'

Ciara's granny left her €20,000 of savings, with the express proviso that she use it to put herself through 'hat-making college'. Ciara's parents want her to be a primary-school teacher who pays off their mortgage so they can spend their money on cruises and possibly retire early. Ciara is not complying with their wishes because she feels that Grandma Lily's instructions should be honoured and because her life's ambition is to be a milliner of some description with her own little hat-elier (see what I did there?) and everything. She is really talented and I wish

I had more call to wear hats because the ones she makes are nothing short of lovely.

'Three more years,' she said grimly.

I nodded.

'Three more years' is kind of our motto at the moment. We share it. Ciara uses it whenever her mum is being all snippy. (Her dad can also be pretty snippy, but he feels more conflicted about completely ignoring Grandma Lily's wishes, seeing as how she gave birth to him back before epidurals were readily available and so on.) I use 'three more years' whenever Fintan is being impossible. Ciara is using it more than me these days, but that might just change now that I am in possession of Mum's diaries.

'Don't judge me based on what you read in there, Prim,' Dad said as he handed the diaries to me. 'What happened between your mother and me was regrettable and I should have acted differently.'

'Like not gotten her pregnant, maybe?'

'Yes. Wait, that's a trick question, isn't it? No. No. NO!'

And then he got stuttery about how he should have done certain things differently but he didn't regret having me and so on until I put him out of his misery by admitting that I was trying to FLUMMOX him.

I love that word, 'flummox'. Ella's mum uses it all the time. This will be my first year of not being taken care of by Mary after school. Instead I will be going to two hours of after-school study. Because it is my post-Junior Cert year and I am now mature enough to spend an extra two hours in the marvellous establishment which I frequent so delightedly every single day of my adolescent life. Except for weekends. And holidays. But that is still a hell of a lot of days. I hope Joel isn't going. Or Karen. They're total besties now, all laughing at each other's stupid jokes and being gay together.

Karen is a lesbian or bisexual or something – I can't really keep track. The above statement comes across a bit bigoty. Unless you know how evil Karen is. Which is kind of why Joel and I are fighting. I did something very wrong and it wasn't nice of me. But I think it is more OK to do something wrong to Karen than it is to do something wrong to other people. Because

She really is and now she and Joel act like *I* am the devil and I amn't, I really truly amn't. I'm just a girl trying to survive in this crazy mixed-up world.

I miss Joel so much, but he won't be my friend any more, until I apologise to Karen again and I already had to apologise to her once and I will not apologise to her any more times until she apologises to me for being a horror. In exactly those words: 'I am sorry I am such a horror, Prim. It was hurtful and wrong of me. I will try not to be in the future.' And then she has to follow it up with being nice to everyone for six months and maybe then we can talk about me maybe drafting something in the line of an apology.

Last year I went through a big phase of wanting to be a cruciverbalist (the people who draft and assemble the crosswords that go in the papers). It still sounds cool, but I'm so sick of hinting what I want and analysing other people's hints at what they want. It is exhausting. I just want to know what Joel wants me to do so this will all be fixed and we will be best friends since Montessori again.

It started because he fancied Kevin, I think. The rift. He really fancied Kevin and I wanted a boyfriend and Kevin seemed like he wanted to be my boyfriend and I fancied him even though he was a LARPer and so forth. Looking back, I can see that I totally backed the wrong horse. Kevin turned out to be a bad idea – not that he was cruel to me or anything, just really, really indecisive about what he wanted from a relationship and bad at texting back. And not kissing other girls. But we never really defined exactly what we were, so I suppose it doesn't really count as cheating. It felt like cheating, though. I was quite hurt. Anyway, even though Kevin isn't gay I totally hi-jacked Joel's crush and made it into my own on-again/off-again dramatic thing that I (admittedly) talked about a lot. Because I was thinking about it a lot. And Ciara kind of encourages that sort of boy-obsession. The analysis of texts and looks and tones of voice.

So Joel felt kind of horrid about that, and sometimes I would kind of break up with Kevin, vowing never to kiss him on sofas, on dance-floors, in his parents' kitchen or behind cinemas again because of that, but I kind of always ended up regretting it and getting back together. Or hooking up in Ciara's parents' walk-in wardrobe at her Sweet Sixteenth house party. We initially went in there to talk, but with Kevin it never really ends with talking. We say things and then there are pauses that we kiss each other to fill. I'm not even sure if we're proper friends, not really. I kind of have always seen him as a kind of sex-object. (Not that we're *having* sex.) First, he was Joel's crush, and then he was my first kiss. Then he was my undefined-sort-of-boyfriend, and now he is my – ex? But somehow he has insinuated himself into our group of friends and now he is a part of the stuff we do. He's still friends with Joel, at least a bit, so he helps me to find out what he (Joel) is up to. I miss just knowing. I miss being able to ask Joel myself.

They're always off doing things together, Karen and Joel. Probably talking about how much better friends they are than he and I could ever have been. They've been to gay bars in town together and everything. Karen knows how to get fake age cards. Karen knows how to get fake everything. I wish I hadn't outed her during big break over the intercom, but I paid my dues and got suspended for a week for bullying, which is rich because she is always bringing up my dead mum and putting me and my friends down, like reminding Ciara about how she used to eat her own hair. Last year at this dance thing we all went to, she actually referred to the way Mum died as 'squishing'. But that doesn't count because it wasn't on school premises and I'm white and straight and incapable of being hate-crimed, even if I wanted to be. Dad was

 with me and I know I was in the wrong and I did do the whole school-imposed apology thing that they made me write to her, but I didn't mean it and I had my fingers crossed the whole time I was writing it, which meant it was all lies and nigh illegible. I did write a real one. But I don't think sending it would sort things.

LETTER TO KAREN draft 24 (UNSENT)

Dear Karen

I am sorry that I outed you. I am not homophobic
and am completely supportive of your lesbionic
identity. I probably should have made this clear when
I discovered you and Nora from TY shifting in that
little alcove made of bins behind the cinema that
people often use for hooking up in because it is private
and provides much-needed shelter from both eyes and
weather. I've used it myself from time to time.

The thing is, Karen, being unsure about your
sexuality, or being full-sure about it and still not
telling people for a variety of reasons, is no excuse
for being heinous. Look at Joel: he is a proud gay man
now, but it wasn't always so. He was once an
ashamed gay man and this made him very grumpy at
times. But he was still nice to people, except his
parents who he often yelled at because he is a
teenager and that is what we teenagers are wont to
do. Are you wont to yell at your parents, Karen?
Because you are certainly wont to yell at other

people's. You called Simone's mum 'a fat-ass' to her face one day because of a lift she had refused you a year and a half ago. This is not the carry-on of a decent human being. And so it was for your lack of decency and not for your surfeit of lesbiosity that I chose to get my revenge on you, albeit in not the nicest of ways.

But revenge, Karen, is never really nice, now, is it? No! It is not. It is bitter and brutal and apparently best served cold, which I never understood until Fintan pointed out that it should be cold because you sit on it and let your anger subside and then, when all your emotions are even and chilly, you act! I did not serve your revenge cold, Karen. If I waited till I was no longer angry at you, I would be waiting till my deathbed. You are the devil and I wish you were dead but I am also sorry.

Sincerely
Primrose Leary

*Sometimes I wish there were two
of me so I could give myself a smather.
Sometimes I wish Fintan and I
had never met at all.*

saw a dead badger on the road this morning on the way to school and it looked like it was sleeping. I have always loved the black and grey and white look of badgers. There's something so sensible about how sturdy and stripy they are. I know they're supposed to be vicious and everything, but because they look like an illustration from a beloved childhood book, I kind of associate them with benevolence and sensible countryside wisdom. Its forepaw was draped halfway across its belly, as though it was snuggling into the side of the road to get comfortable. It wasn't, though. It was dead. I didn't expect the sight of it to have such an effect on me. I actually felt like I had seen a dead unicorn or something. I never expected that badgers lurked in grassy bits of Dublin. An omen, Sorrel (Mum's co-best friend, my sort of auntie) would call that.

Mum's diaries are kind of hard to process. I understand now why Dad left them till I was sixteen. They're lovely in a way, but I'm reading through the time she was with Fintan at the moment, and it's difficult. Because she

Quote from Prim's mum's diary

is so young and even though she is older than I am now, it's not by much and I want to protect her from her future. How strong she will have to be, how brave! I don't know if I could be as brave and strong as Mum was but, at the same time, I kind of hope I would be. If a crisis happened, I would love to be able to deal with it gracefully. It is REALLY weird to be reading about the times that led to my conception. I mean, I know that they were together, but it kind of blows my mind that there was a time when my mum actually fancied my dad. Like, seriously fancied. The way I feel about Kevin sometimes when I am in a charitable mood or daydreaming out the window during class.

I think I am going to write another apology letter to Karen. I will read it out to Joel's voicemail and see if it is good enough to make him be friends with me again.

LETTER TO KAREN draft 47 (UNSENT)

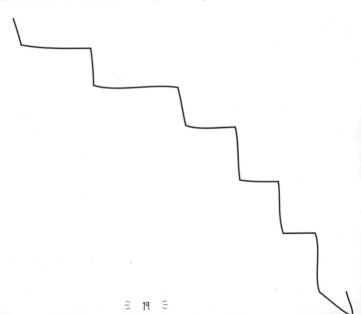

Dear Karen

I am sorry that Joel is not my friend any more and, by extension, I am sorry for what I did to you. Well, actually, I am genuinely sorry for what I did. Not because it hurt your feelings, because I think we both know you don't have a soul and your feelings are impermeable. God, I hate you. But I love Joel and so I am ready to admit that I did a bad thing, the kind of thing someone like you wouldn't think twice about. It galls me so much that you are being perceived as a victim of bullying, Karen, when you can make a first year wet herself with a single pointed glance. Anyway, I am sorry that you are alive and that I was mean to you.

Sincerely,
Primrose

I miss him terribly. I don't have a lot of family and I don't want to lose the bits of it I have left. Especially Joel because he is a member of the family you build for yourself – the friends and allies you can call at three o'clock in the morning if you really need them. I rarely call people, though, when I'm in that sort of headspace. Because I don't like throwing my problems all over them and I know you can't rely on friends to, like, provide you with happiness. That has to come from yourself. Or something. Not that I'm an authority on happiness or anything, although I have my moments. Usually when I'm happy.

Joel is always such a huge part of my summer, to the point that we actually resent each other's holidays with family. Not that Fintan ever takes me anywhere – his holidays tend to be work-related. He should step up and fork out because I really want to go to Paris and walk around it in ballet pumps and a stripy jumper, pretending that I am an artist or some sort of muse to an artist or in an indie band with a cult following. Fintan isn't sure about Paris, because he associates it with his lost love, Hedda, who is now married to a human rights lawyer named Gallen, whom I have never seen and always picture as an elf.

I wish that Fintan had been nicer to my mum and not flirted with her housemate, Gillian, whom I have never met but will probably automatically hate if I ever do meet her because she was a disloyal and scheming friend. I wonder if that is how Joel feels about me.

Why is Fintan even with me? He doesn't think I'm half as interesting as the stock market or the other women he insists on flirting with even when I'm in the room. It's like he wants me to never be too sure of him. In fairness to him, it is working a charm.

Dad is kind of with me yet against me on the whole Karen thing. He is with me because he understands that she is the devil, yet he thinks that I went 'far too far', what with announcing her sexual orientation over the intercom. He thinks that the teachers realise that Karen is evil incarnate, but came down hard on me because they were worried that me 'breaking in' (how is it breaking if the door isn't even locked?) to the principal's office and 'commandeering' (how is it commandeering if no-one else was even using it?) the intercom for purposes that were 'not school-related' (I could argue this one, but – honestly – fair enough) would set a worrying precedent. It totally did, too. While I was suspended (but before Ms Cleary put the padlock on the office door) a second-year invited the whole school to her 'free gaff' over the intercom in the hopes of popularity.

My outing of Karen, while hardly a public service announcement, had a sort of an odd justice to it. I did not do it for personal gain. I did it to get back at the devil. Which is kind of in keeping with my school's Catholic ethos. If anything I should be

I am not looking forward to September. So it's a good thing I have two and a bit months. One positive thing about the whole Karen situation was that I didn't stress about the Junior Cert at all. By the time all of that nonsense went down we were just going over stuff in most of the classes anyway, so it's not like I lost out. It was horrible not talking to Joel during the exams, though, because he'd be there talking about however things had gone for him and I'd pipe up and join in and he would just cut me dead. He'd do this thing where his eyes would sweep over me as if I wasn't there and it felt absolutely horrible.

Ciara was no help with the Joel situation. 'I need to focus,

Prim,' she kept saying whenever I wanted to talk about things that weren't whatever-exam-we-were-having-that-day-related. I mean, she'd talk about it for a while – she didn't, like, cut me dead or anything – but her heart wasn't in it. I could tell she really wished that, instead of asking her how to make Joel be my friend again and analysing his every mid-exam bathroom break, I would shut up and start pop-quizzing her on notable Portuguese explorer Ferdinand Magellan. Who kind of reminds me of Fintan, if Fintan was a fifteenth-century man, with a beard and a ridiculous velvet hat.

Ferdinand Magellan is hotter than Christopher Columbus, but not by much. And, to be fair, there are very few people in all of history who are not more attractive than Christopher Columbus. The most handsome explorer of them all is charismatic conquistador Hernando Cortés. But you couldn't hit that and live with yourself because he was properly evil and massacred the Aztecs and stuff.

Fintan spent twenty-five pounds on a tie yesterday.

What a ridiculous man he is!

(Still fancy the pants off him, though.)

Dad was mad stressed from work today. When he came home to find me reading Mum's diaries at the kitchen table he got all awkward. Which he should be, because he mostly comes off as an idiot in them. Whenever I find myself getting angry at past-Fintan, I take a break and read the diaries from long before she met him. (Fourteen-year-old Mum had yet to kiss a boy, much less a stupid man who didn't appreciate how wonderful she was.) It is weird, seeing bits of your mum most people never get to see. She hated business studies and loved English. She had a crush on a boy called Ruairí, who worked in the local shop. He was two years older than her and already had a girlfriend, called Maeve.

It is weird having little fragments of your mother all stored up to dole out to yourself. I was kind of hoping there'd be deep dark secrets and some sort of guide to how to live your life out as a decent human being enclosed with the diaries. No such luck, though. Mum seemed to mess up almost as much as me. Except she hasn't been suspended for homophobic bullying yet.

Quote from Prim's mum's diary

I think, back in the day, homophobic bullying was kind of normal. It was actually illegal for a man to make love to another man. It would be horrible to be put in prison just because you fell in love with someone or met someone you really wanted to do stuff with. And they didn't have a special sexy prison for people who were convicted of doing stuff that shouldn't even be illegal at all. They'd just be bunged right into normal prison with the murderers and rapists and drug dealers and what-not.

I would totally have visited Joel if he had been arrested and put in prison. In a way, if we lived back in the days when Mum was young and he was arrested for sexy times, it would be kind of a good thing for our friendship. Because he would have to talk to me then, if only to complain about how unfair the situation was. I am a bit Machiavellian sometimes. Which is probably a good thing because I quoted him in my history paper.

I think I might be in love with Fintan.

Either that or I really want to

sleep with him some more. Definitely

one or the other.

MESSAGE TO KAREN draft 92

Dear Karen
I was wrong to do what I did. And I am very sorry
that I did it. Please tell Joel you forgive me so he
will be my friend again.
Prim

I private-messaged Karen this and when I went back to
see if she'd replied I realised she had blocked me. She
must have blocked me as soon as she read it. I'm so
angry I could punch her in the face. Again. Oh, God,
that really does make me sound like a bully, doesn't it?
Even though it was almost three years ago and I was
defending Ella and it didn't really hurt Karen at all.

I can throw a really good punch now, though. I could
probably do some real damage after all those kick-boxing
lessons I took last term on the advice of my therapist.
I kind of like the way Caroline gives me head-fixing

homework. Like – I go to kick-boxing because endorphins will make me happier and punching and kicking will be a violent thing I can do that does not harm me or anyone else. Not that I've ever harmed anyone. Except my own hand when I made a complete hames of punching Karen.

I kind of used to cut myself, though. Not a lot. Just some-

times it was a thing I did instead of being sad and

angry. Or as well as being sad and

angry. I am still sad and angry a lot of the time, but I don't go at my legs and stomach any more.

I still think about it sometimes, though

Like the way people think about someone else's unopened box of chocolates in their fridge. Like I shouldn't but I kind of really want to. What is it about being blocked on a social networking site that's so IRRITATING? I'm surprised Joel hasn't blocked me yet. He did un-friend me though. Which hurt a lot. Because I felt, like, he can't just un-friend me – we've been friends since we were four years old. That is, like, three-quarters of our lives. It seems really dramatic. (Although my life does tend to swing that way, what with the cemetery break-ins and the self-harming and the manslaughtered mum.)

I love my friends, though. I don't see how you can just cut someone out of your life (except for Kevin, whom I probably should, from a kissing point of view at least). I am a nice person and he knows full well that I'm not homophobic. I've helped him through so many things around his sexual identity and him being OK with it and other people being OK with it and other people not being OK with it because they are stupid and wrong. Dad took him for post coming-out-related-drama

for God's sake.

Crepes are the most supportive food there is, next to toffee-pops. Joel is good at being angry and mean, but even if he was the kind of angry that involves yelling at me, I could win him around. I know I could. I'm very good at being friends with Joel. But he has never not talked to me before. I've always been the one who didn't talk to him. I don't like this shift in the balance of friend-power. It makes me feel like things might actually be over for us. And that doesn't bear thinking about and leads to over-analytical thought spirals where I try to rewrite the past by regretting it and am no good to anyone.

I think getting with Kevin was a big mistake, friendship-wise. Friends shouldn't kiss other friends' crushes, even if there is no actual way that the friend with the crush could get with his or her crush and the friend who is supposed to get away is feeling vulnerable and also a little bit tempted to keep kissing the first ever boy to show any sexual interest in her in the hopes of getting an actual boyfriend. I really wanted Kevin to be my first boyfriend. I wanted him to like me as much as Syzmon likes Ciara and to want to do stuff with me that we both enjoyed. Sadly, he is a teenage boy. (I know Syzmon is as well, but he doesn't really count because I suspect Ciara and he are mutants whose super power is happy-ever-after-getting and monogamy.) And I don't want 'a boyfriend'. I want the real thing. Love, or something that I think is love right now. Someone who likes me and wants me and thinks that the stupid stuff I say and sometimes do is somehow charming. Someone who will be as close to me as Joel is but who I will also want to do sex things with and to. Not loads of sex things. But some definite sex things. Cosy, consensual, mutually enjoyable sex things.

Reading Mum's old romances has given me strong guidelines as to how it should be. Except without the brawny (yet weirdly progressive in terms of open-mindedness and personal hygiene) Viking protagonist kidnapping me and taking me to his keep

as a hostage, with whom he ultimately falls in love. Not that that isn't nice to think about sometimes, but I have no desire to actually be kidnapped, even if it is by a sexy Viking with a booming laugh who will shower me with mead and gilded pleasures for years to come. However, I do want to have a love story, even if it's a tragic one. I don't think anyone will ever make me as sad as Dad made Mum, though.

I think that my losing her has made the worst sad happen early and maybe everything else will hurt, but not as much, because after that it all has to be less. I can't feel any more grief than I already have. I think my body would refuse it and shut down and just stop responding to stimuli. I'm not sure, though. It's just a feeling. A hunch. I think I'm right, though. I think that I am bullet-proof somehow, in terms of drama. Except for the whole not-talking-to-Joel thing, which makes me cry like maybe once a week.

It has been six weeks since I walked in on Fintan with his tongue down Gillian's throat. She's going to move out as soon as she finds someone else to take the room. I would like to kill the both of them. But I am not going to because I am the bigger person here.

Past-Dad is a horrible man. He has been steadily making moves on Mum's house-mate, and Mum has been pretending not to notice, while totally noticing and obsessing about it. She's just walked in on him with Gillian and he's pretending that it's nothing but it is very, very something indeed. It is all quite sad. I feel kind of weird about talking to Dad about the cheating, though, because it's all over and done with and in the past and he has been a pretty good dad to me, even if he is hardly ever a good boyfriend to anyone. I don't like to think of him being a friend-groper, though. Shudder. I wish I could talk to Joel about it, but I suppose I'll just have to hold it in and bring it up next time I see Caroline.

Quote from Prim's mum's diary

Which is Thursday week. I wonder if I can hold it in that long? I'd tell Ciara, but I'm not sure she could keep it secret and also she has a big thing about cheaters and how they are scum and all that, so I think she would probably get quite snotty with Dad if she knew about his historical handsy-ness.

I love reading Mum's diaries. I love that there are bits of her that are left to me, that I can still learn from and love. But at the same time, there is a reason that parents don't share everything with their kids. And that reason is because they probably don't want to gross them out completely. And also their entitlement to a private life, etc.

Dear Joel
I have found some scandalous gossip from the past in Mum's diary. If you will accept my apology to Karen and be my friend again I will tell you what it is.
Prim

Dear Prim
I can't BELIEVE you're using your dead mother's diaries to blackmail me. That's low, even for you. You are a selfish person and I am better off without you in my life.
Joel

Don't be like that.

I am the way I am – a proud gay man, and your homophobic bullying of Karen and general bad treatment of me in other ways has made me realise how much you were holding me back.

I have never not supported your sexual identity. I love you and I am so proud of you. If you are talking about the Kevin thing, you know how much I tortured myself over that. I wish I had not outed Karen, I was not think-ing clearly – she just makes me so angry. I shouldn't have done it and definitely wouldn't have if I knew it was going to be the catalyst for a rift between us. You are my family, Joel. Even if you decide never to talk to me again, I will not stop being here for you.
Your friend (even if you aren't mine)
Prim

That last one didn't deliver, because he had blocked me. I'm going to print it out and post it to him, though. I will have the last word. Even if it could result in embar-rassing feelingsy notes being read out loud in a silly voice to horrible Karen.

Sorrel sent me out for Tampax from the corner shop and something dreadful occurred to me. It's been about two months since I had my period.

~~JjjjjjjjjjjjjjjjFUCK!!!~~

'm over it. I'm so over it that I am planning on getting a new boy best friend to replace Joel. I am holding auditions that the boys involved do not know are auditions. I am meeting Kevin for ice-cream on Monday and going for tea with Felix on Thursday. Then there is the wild card, Robb from the maths revision course Dad sent me on at Easter to get me out of the house. Robb has two bees and goes to boarding school. He is not around during term time, but we banter a lot through the medium of the Internet and I am meeting him on Wednesday. Ciara is very excited about these auditions.

'Maybe instead of finding a new Joel, you will find **TRUE LOVE.**'

I have capitalised **TRUE LOVE** here because that is how Ciara thinks of it, like it is more important than anything. Now that she is sixteen, she and Syzmon have been getting more serious. She isn't ready to sleep with him yet but they are having quite a nice time of it, nonetheless.

Quote from Prim's mum's diary

'I am not going to find **TRUE LOVE**, Ciara.' I capitalised true love a bit mockingly, to imply my contempt for the concept.

People are too stupid to be 'meant to be' together. The best we can hope for is that you will make a friend you want to do things with and isn't boring or mean to you. I am not looking for love like my silly mother was at my age. I am only looking for a new Joel because getting the old one to talk to me is apparently impossible.

I wouldn't mind if I were to meet someone nice, though.

THIS IS MY CHECKLIST OF
WANTS IN A BOYFRIEND:

1. Is funny. 2. Is someone I fancy.

3. Is not mean to me. 4. Does not bore me.

5. Is not related to the man
who killed my mother.

(Number 5 was added out of necessity.
Stupid handsome Mac.)

And even so, Ciara – who has a list she keeps adding to that now has

234

items on it – thinks I am too picky.

I really don't want to be pregnant.

I'm not going to have an abortion or anything.

But I just thought I'd mention it ...

hy am I still sad all the time, even though it's summer? It isn't all about Joel. It isn't all about Mum. Some of it is just about me. There is a heaviness in my stomach and it's been there so long that sometimes I wonder if I was born with it. I don't think I was, though. I think that I remember being light.

I am meeting Kevin tomorrow and I am excited as well as sad. I need to be very brave around Kevin. He makes me wish I had an amazing new boyfriend. So I could be all, 'Kevin, have you met my amazing new boyfriend and part-time soul-mate? His name is Cliff Dirtbike and he lives up to it every day of his life. Cliff, honey, show Kevin how you can lift me over your head as though I were no heavier than a blossom.'

I like the idea of Cliff. I'd probably call him something else, though. If he were real, I would not be thinking about the smell of Kevin's neck and the way his hands are way bigger than mine. I would only think of Kevin platonically, if Cliff existed. Where are you, Cliff? I need you to help me resist Kevin-shaped temptation!!

Quote from Prim's mum's diary

Fintan is supporting me through this. Those were his words. As if it were a postgrad or an illness. As though he had nothing at all to do with this human being growing in my stomach.

Kevin-shaped temptation will be very easy to resist this summer, as it happens. He called to inform me that has a new girlfriend, Siobhán from my year, and will no longer be available for ice-cream. Siobhán is friends with Karen. She only talks to us when Karen is being mean to her. People seem to gravitate to me and Ciara when they are in danger of being pushed out of Karen's group, for some reason. I don't know why. It's not like we're that nice and friendly. We're kind of in-jokey and Karen-hating and quiet around people we don't know.

Kevin and Siobhán have been going out for a week and a half. He 'thought I should know'. He still wants to hang out with me. He 'values our friendship'. I wonder if he asked her to be his girlfriend. I wonder what it is about her that screams 'girlfriend', as opposed to 'furiously-make-out-in-random-places-with-friend-who-is-a-girl'. I've never had a proper boyfriend, really. Kevin is as close as it has got. Who will tell me I'm pretty and give me cidery kisses and sometimes unhook my bra by way of a joke now? I am not sad, exactly. But I am feeling some definite feelings about this and they are not all good.

Quote from Prim's mum's diary

I rang Joel to tell him about Kevin and Siobhán. He didn't pick up but I left him a voicemail. A really rambly one that cut out just at the part where I was, like, 'I miss you so much every single day' and about to cry. I hate Karen so much. I hate her. Why does she have to steal my best friend? I wish I could steal something belonging to her. Like her phone, or kidneys. That'd show her who the boss was. I don't want to be the boss, though. I don't know what I want to be, except Joel's friend.

When I got home from being broken up with for another girl by someone who didn't even care enough about me to be my boyfriend, Fintan and Sorrel were in the kitchen. Sorrel has been coming over a bit recently. She is short of money because she has gone back to college to learn how to be a midwife, which she has wanted to do for ages. Literally. Mum even wrote about it a bit in her diaries. Fintan has been paying her to clean the house, mind me every now and then and give him Indian head massages. Sorrel is a woman of many skills. She had made some banana bread. It was amazing.

'What's wrong, Prim?'

'Nothing, Sorrel.'

'Are you sure?' said Fintan, pushing his eyebrows close together in a show of fatherly concern.

'Yes.'

'She's not sure at all, Sorrel. Listen to the grumpy tone of her.'

'Shut up, Fintan.' I don't know why I told him to shut up. It was clear it was going to annoy him. Gah.

'Don't you dare tell me to shut up, you little rip. I'd send you to your room only I'm very relaxed and forgiving at the moment after my Indian head massage.'

Sorrel looked really pleased.

I informed him that, yes, I was in a bad mood but that I did not want to talk about it.

'Do you want to eat banana bread and drink tea and talk about other things?' he asked, scratching his moustache in that way he does when he's not sure what to do with me.

'Yes. Yes, I do.'

One thing I like about Sorrel is that she never pushes. Also, she is genuinely interested in my life and friends and stuff. She doesn't come over only out of loyalty to Mum. She wants to hang out with me as well. This is nice and means I will forgive her almost anything and indulge her when she talks about things like 'cleanses' and 'meditation circles'.

I'm still not sure about the moon-cup she gave me for my sixteenth birthday, though. It might be a bridge too far,

which is a bridge past the acceptable place for bridges to be. Whether it is an overly sharey bridge or an overly gross bridge or an overly judgey bridge, it is not a particularly welcome one. All the other bridges laugh at it behind its back. The reason that Sorrel's gift was a bridge too far is hard to explain without sounding ungrateful. Which I swear I'm not. Just a little weirded out because it was a bit ... um ... *intimate*. A moon-cup is a sort of silicone cup that you place inside your lady garden when it is that special time of the month. It collects all the lady-blood and instead of throwing it out when it gets full, you just empty and rinse it. It is more environmentally friendly than tampons or pads, but it is also a little creepy when given as a birthday present by a grown-up person to whom you have to write a thank-you card. How would I even phrase that, like? She has not asked me what I think of it yet, which shows that she has at least some level of cop-on. I would have preferred an Indian head massage, to be honest. And those skeeve me out a great deal.

Why can't I fall for people who are nice to me? Why do people who are mean exert this kind of power over me, where I will bend over backwards to please them? When my baby comes, I want it to have a stable, healthy, normal life.

I have to stop being so stupid.

Kevin having a girlfriend impacts very little on me one way or another. I was never going to be with him again. So it is probably actually a good thing. Siobhán is friends with Karen also, so the two of them probably deserve each other. So it is definitely a good thing that he is out of bounds and forbidden as a result of belonging to another. He was already out of bounds and forbidden as a result of being detrimental to my mental health anyway. I am going to be mature about this and not try to seduce him at house parties.

Syzmon is having a house party in a fortnight's time when his parents go back to Slovakia for a month. He is joining them for two weeks, but he also has a free house for two weeks. Syzmon is hard-working and responsible. His parents trust him not to trash the place. And he won't. But he will be holding a series of shindigs.

Shindigs are what Ciara calls parties. Sometimes she talks like a little old lady. This is part of Grandma Lily's

Quote from Prim's mum's diary

legacy. Along with a shedload of cash and Ciara saying the rosary sometimes when she is feeling panicked. Ciara is pretty sure she does not believe in God, but she is very pro-the-mystical-power-of-the-rosary. She got me a bracelet of it for my birthday. It is red and has green and yellow enamel flowers on the beads. I like it a lot, but I haven't worn it yet because I'm worried that people will think that I'm religious if I do. They probably won't. You can get crucifixes in Topshop. They're not exclusively sold to believers or anything.

I do go to mass with Dad sometimes. We light a candle for Mum at the end, normally, and that is my favourite part, when people have trickled out and we are mainly by ourselves. Churches are pretty. It's a pity they are full of mass. Mum wasn't too gone on mass herself. Her parents were religious and they kind of went mad at her when she got pregnant with me. They got over themselves a little bit later on, when I was small and cute, but they were never a great support to her. In her diaries, she is so afraid of how much work it will be and scared she'll have to do it by herself. And she *will* have to do it mostly by herself, because that is what my life was till she died. Her and me and, on the weekends, Fintan. Well, on the weekends that he wasn't busy. He makes a pretty good full-time dad, actually. It is a pity he didn't try to be one before Mum died, especially when I was small and loads of work and she could have done with a break.

He paid for minders and things when she was at college. That isn't very romantic. But Mum thought it was a nice thing to do and felt bad about being, like, beholden to him and all of his money or whatever. It is strange reading her diaries. Because I know how it ends with Dad. And how it ends with me. She knew she'd love me, but she didn't want me yet. But it's good that she had me when she did, because she died and if I had been smaller I wouldn't have had as much time with her as I did.

I am meeting Robb with two bees tomorrow. We are going to have tea and cake and hang out in town, looking at things. It will probably be boring. I will either not be able to think of things to say, or say too many things and things that are the wrong thing. Like, 'Is that your favourite jumper and, if so, why?'

It's not like I want to hook up with him or anything. But I would like a boyfriend, if only just to show Kevin that I am in demand and worth fancying. And also to show Joel that there are interesting things going on in my life, even when he is not there to make me be more out-going and fun. I always feel more fun when Joel's around because we make each other laugh so much. I think I will wear my short dark-red mini-dress with the cap sleeves and the brown buttons. It makes me look older, and also kind of pretty. And I'll wear my hair down. Probably.

RO

I know I'll love the baby when it comes.

But I'm clever enough to know that I will probably fail it. And what kind of father will Fintan make?

obb with two bees and I had a very pleasant day together. I said some awkward things to him, but he said some to me as well. Loads of anecdotes about boarding school. And the jolly japes they get up to in boarding school. Japes are pranks, jokes, Trickery and Adventures. 'Japes' is a very boarding-school word, I think. Other very boarding-school words include 'midnight feasts', 'prep', 'tuck shop', 'boater', 'jolly', 'dormitory', 'san', 'frolic', 'prankster', 'prig', 'prefect', 'head girl', 'good show' and 'parental abandonment'.

While he is busy being a ridiculous Enid Blyton-style 'boarder', Robb does tend to miss his family, but boarding school has given him a sort of new family. Made of teenagers. He makes it sound delightful, but I still don't think that I would like it very much. I sometimes like to be by myself. I told him that, and he was all, 'We have a room for that!' It is called the Reflection Room, apparently. I don't think I have ever met anyone who loves school before. He misses it a bit. OK, a lot.

Apart from that he's really normal, though. He paid for my cake and we walked around and sat by the river while he had a smoke. He smokes. Everyone in boarding school smokes. I had a cigarette to keep him company. And also slightly to impress him. Because smoking does look cool. And smokers love the taste of cigarettes, so I thought that if he kissed me and I tasted like cigarettes, he might think I was delicious. He didn't kiss me, though.

But we did talk a lot about ducks and he told me that duck-junk is the same size as man-junk. He didn't say 'duck-junk', though, he said 'penises'. I will never look at a duck the same way again. We both got a bit awkward after he mentioned penises. Because it felt like the image of one was dangling between us in the air. So I told him about how all the swans in England belong to the queen, but that the ones in Ireland just belong to themselves and then we talked about how cool it would be to have an army of swans at your disposal because swans are quite vicious and would be handy in a fight. Robb doesn't have any pets. His mother is very house-proud and he's at boarding school for most of the year, so it's not like he has time to take care of a dog or anything. I told him about Roderick but I think he might not have got how close to him I was because he took the stance that rats are full of diseases (LIE) and that they are incontinent (LIE), so they pee everywhere and their pee is poisonous and odourless and deadly (LIE). I think his house-proud mother might be responsible for his many misconceptions about rats.

If Roderick were still alive, I would have totally invited Robb over to play with him. As it was, I just got a bit what Ciara calls 'debatey' and took him down point for point and would not let him be even a little bit right about things that he was clearly wrong about.

Sample exchange between Robb and me on the subject of rats:

Robb: 'Let's agree to disagree.'
Me: 'Let's agree that you're WRONG.'
Robb: 'I'm not wrong.'
Me: 'Have you ever even seen a rat?'
Robb: 'Only in a pet-shop.'
Me: 'So you'll accept that I know more about rats than you.'
Robb: 'You know more about your pet rat than I do, but that's not to say you know more about rats in general.'
Me: 'Have you read On Rat-care?'
Robb: 'No.'
Me: 'Or How to Make Your Rat Happy: An Owner's Manual?'
Robb: 'No.'
Me: 'Or, God, ANY of them? I've got, like, twelve books on rat-minding. People kept getting them for me for birthdays and things.'
Robb: 'I've read Mrs Frisby and the Rats of Nimh.'
Me: 'Doesn't count.'
Robb (quietly): 'I didn't think it would.'

I went for the bus soon after. We arranged to meet again because we both want to see the new Batman film. I don't think that Robb with two bees is my TRUE LOVE, though. I do not even slightly want to hook up with him. I do kind of want *him* to want to hook up with *me*, though. But that's more about self-esteem boosting than because there's any real spark. I can't believe he loves school and hates rats. I want to change his mind about both of those things. Summer project! I'll send him back to boarding school a rat-loving shadow of his former self.

EEP.

My dad called me a whore. I'm not a whore.
But when your father calls you one, no matter how
innocent and un-slappery you are, you sort of feel like
one. All dirty on the inside. Cheap and stupid.

S o I met up with Felix today. I wasn't sure why he wanted to. Because we don't really hang out together, except for when Ella is around. He kind of goes out with us a lot, because he likes to watch her and make sure that she is OK. This is partly adorable and responsible and partly creepy. Because even though she has autism, Ella can totally handle herself. If she gets irritated or wants to repeat things or do weird movements with her hands, she usually just goes to the loo to do it and then comes back in a better mood or rings Mary to pick her up.

Felix was looking well. He's kind of the polar opposite of Kevin. All lanky and lean and with hair that is messy and ruffled looking. His fingers are long and his nails are short. His hands have little rough patches on them from playing the guitar. I want to know what those little rough patches feel like, to run my pale, stubby fingers over them and have him smile at me and like my touch.

Quote from Prim's mum's diary

Dad was **AAAGES** pottering about the place before he dropped me in, though. I would have been so much quicker getting the bus. But he was insistent that he give me a lift. I think doing stuff for me every now and then makes him feel like a better parent than he actually is. That's unfair. He's a pretty good parent. He just hasn't had as much practice as Mum had. He was asking me about Mum's diaries again.

'I hope I'm not coming off too badly in them,' he said in a fake jovial manner. 'The last thing I'd need would be for you to start hating me or anything.'

'To be honest, Dad, I'm not planning on starting to hate you. That's not what would worry me about the whole situation.'

'Oh?'

I made a triangle with my fingers, the way Caroline sometimes does when she's explaining something. 'You see, I read somewhere that young women who have grown up with absent or largely absent father-figures often gravitate towards men who resemble their fathers.'

'Oh.' Fintan did not like where this was going.

'So, even though I will try to avoid it – because who would want the sort of half-assed relationship you inflicted on poor Mum? – I might not be able to.'

'You probably would, though.'

'I don't know, Dad.'

'I wouldn't let you get into that sort of situation.'

'To be honest, I probably wouldn't tell you about it. Until I had to because of the pregnancy. Mum certainly didn't tell her parents about you, and as I recall you encouraged that.'

Fintan looked down. 'I probably did, yeah.'

'So when I come home pregnant by some middle-aged creep who couldn't care less about me, you will be in no position to admonish him, or me. And that is why I am not doing the recrimination thing now. Life will do the recrimination thing to you at a later date. And you will have no-one but yourself to blame. It's like that poster Mum used to have in the kitchen, Fintan. "Children learn what they live."'

'I should never have given you those diaries,' he muttered, still glowering at his bespoke Italian loafers.

'Keeping them to yourself would have changed nothing. It is like Sorrel says, Dad. Our destinies are

written
in the
stars.

Ooh! Maybe she could be my midwife!'

I do not believe a word of this, of course, but I am kind of angry at him for what happened back in the day, while still aware that he is actually a nice man deep down, and not wanting to pick a big row with him that will just make both of us miserable and grumpy until we make up. I probably would pick a fight with him if Joel were still my friend. But he isn't. And I need all the friends I can get. Is it weird and gross that my creepy, older-than-middle-aged Dad is one of my friends now, kind of? It is, isn't it? I am a freak.

Felix, however, is not a freak, just charmingly off-beat. He was reading and listening to music when I walked into the café, in an ensemble I had chosen because it made me look curvy and grown-up without being too try-hard. I think. I was also wearing mascara, eyeliner and lip-gloss, so there was that. I have a big spot in one corner of my nose and it is really sore and itchy and I had lathered it in concealer but that just made things worse, so I had wiped it off and it was there, looming out at the world like a bright-red monster. I was wearing a flowery skirt, a ripped up black Metallica T-shirt (I don't really like Metallica, but I do really like skeletons riding motorcycles and black T-shirts that suit me), lacy black tights and beat-up-looking ankle boots. My hair was down and there may have been some straightening involved.

'So ... hi.' Felix shrugged his shoulders and blinked at me.

'Hi.'

We ordered. I got tea and a scone. He got coffee (black) and a brownie. He said that he missed seeing me every day and stuff, and asked how I was getting on. I said that I was getting on OK. Still fighting with Joel.

And Felix said, 'About that ...'

And I said, 'What?'

And then he told me something that made me forget about the spot in the corner of my nose and how I wanted to amaze him. Something that has been worrying me ever since.

Joel has a boyfriend now. A man. A proper, out-of-school, out-of-college, job-having *man*. And Felix doesn't think that that's OK.

'I don't want you to think I'm being homophobic or judgemental or anything, Prim,' he said and his voice was sleepy and emphatic at the same time and I want to do all of the things with and to him. 'I was wondering whether or not to say it to you at all, but then I thought of when you rang me when he was in first year and getting bullied and I thought about Ella and if she were going out with someone so much older, how I'd feel. Or if *you* were, even.'

I'd like to think Felix would be more OK with the concept of me dating an older guy once he realises that the older guy is him and that WE ARE IN LOVE. So in love. Getting side-tracked. Back to Joel.

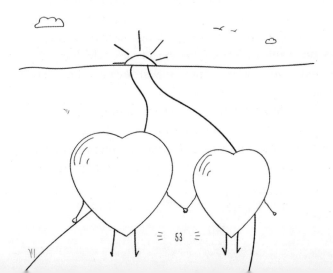

I nodded slowly, resisting the urge to triangle my fingers at him. 'I think you made the right call, Felix. But I don't know what to do about it, really.'

'Neither do I. I mean, it's none of my business ...' He shook his head helplessly. 'I'd just hate to see him hurt, you know?'

'Me too.'

And I really would. I mean, I was so cut up about Kevin and that was hardly even a relationship at all. I felt like he was using me sometimes and that was not a pleasant feeling. If he were older, I think that the potential for feeling used would sky-rocket somewhat. Actually, I don't think. I actually know. Reading Mum's diaries has taught me that older men are not wise life-choices until the two of ye are actual proper adults, and even then you should probably share a decade. So a nine-year difference max.

Joel's man-friend's name is Duncan. That is a very inoffensive name for a paedophile to have. And he is technically a paedophile. I mean, Joel is only sixteen still. You're not allowed to have sex till you're seventeen. So, basically, if this Duncan's slipping it to Joel, that'd be, like, *rape*. Or at the very least against-the-law sex. Not to be alarmist or anything. But it is a concern. It feels really weird to think of rape as something that can happen to a friend. I mean, I know technically it could happen to anyone. But underage people with overage boyfriends have to be at a higher risk of it.

Felix thinks I should be concerned too, obviously. Or he wouldn't have contacted me. But what can I do? I mean, I could tell Liam and Anne, but that would make me even more the bad guy than I am already. And Joel would see it as a betrayal even though it comes from a place of wanting him not to be taken advantage of.

Because, I mean, when Mum was eighteen she went out with my dad and they had me. Joel's two years away from being her age then. But even when she was eighteen and older and wiser and everything than Joel, I can tell Mum wasn't ready for the hurt of being someone's second best. For not being good enough for some things, but plenty good enough for others. Dad used her, and it's not OK to do that to a person. It wasn't just the Gillian thing: he even hit on Sorrel once, and Mum was so embarrassed because she thought that if she could make herself enough for him to love that wouldn't happen, and as I read my heart is breaking for her. And I don't want that to happen to my Joel. He has enough to cope with without the extra hurting all piled on top of other hurts he has from being bullied and things. Things include the stupid thing I did to Karen too. I didn't mean for it to hurt him but still it did and I'm not sure if there's a way to fix it. Even if there is, I think it might be like a teapot when the handle breaks and is stuck back on. The join will still be visible, you know. The little scar.

Felix's eyes are dark and his eyebrows crook when he's worried. I didn't know what to say and I looked at his hands playing with his sugar packet. He doesn't take sugar in his coffee but he played with the little paper cylinder that comes upon the saucer anyway, ratting the paper a little, bending and straightening it. Not meeting my eye.

'How is the band going?' I asked.

'OK.'

His eyes were darting and I could tell he wanted to leave. But I wanted him to stay and so I asked him question after question. Questions with answers I don't even care about or want. His voice isn't exactly deep, but there is a full quality to it. A certainty. It is a voice of trust and bedtime stories. I want to be tucked in by him, to be told that everything will be OK. I wonder how many years I have spent wishing he would see me as a girl and not as a child who is Ella's friend.

My nails were covered in midnight polish, darkest blue and chipped to hell, and I picked what was left right off my little finger rather than look up at him.

'What should I do, Felix? About Joel? I don't know what to do.'

'Me neither. That's why I passed it on to you.'

'It's a hard one.'

'Yeah.'

'I wish I could talk to him, but now he hates me.'

'Because of the Karen thing?'

'I think it grew from Kevin, as it happens.'

'Oh.'

Felix doesn't like Kevin very much. He thinks that he is fake, and kind of posey. I wouldn't know only Ella told me so and she doesn't lie ... Ella is a very moral person. She is kind to small and fragile things.

'Are you and Kevin still ...?' asked Felix, like he cares.

'No. He has another girlfriend now. Not that I was his girlfriend officially.'

'It still matters,' he said, like he gets it.

'It's fine,' I said. 'I don't even care. I mean, I do. But I shouldn't. And it was probably good enough for me. You shouldn't hook up with people your friends like like that. I mean, it isn't kind. It wasn't kind of me. And now I'm being punished for it or something. Between the two of them. I mean, Kevin and Joel. I'm getting sick of being pushed away.'

'Well, if you ever need to talk or anything,' he said, and I could tell he was only saying it to be nice, only saying it because I've puked my feelings out at him and what else do you say to someone who is full of sad and wanting so to not be any more?

'Thanks,' I said. And then, 'I'd better go.'

'Let me know how it goes. With Joel. What you decide to do,' he said.

And I said that I would and then I went to catch the bus and think until my brain was sick from thinking.

What

am

I

going to do

at all,

at all?

LETTER TO KAREN draft 123

Dear Karen

Have you ever been properly sad? The kind of sad that probably won't get better? Maybe you have. I do not know you really. Please let Joel be my friend again, Karen. I miss him terribly.

Primrose

Sorrel says if you use almond oil
every single day you won't get stretch marks.

haven't cut myself in ages. But there are times I really, really want to. There are lines on my hips, ridges. Little scars I made upon my body and I look at them tonight and want to open them back up and let the blood eke out and concentrate on something bad that is on the outside of my body and not the inside. I wish I were a better person than I am. I wish that I were very, very different. I scratch at the nose-spot until it blooms a red disgusting thing. All the pus picked out. It won't go down for ages if you pick. I think it is the lesser of two evils. If I am going to dig something out of myself, I'd rather it was that

Quote from Prim's mum's diary

Fintan is thinking about taking up yoga. Sorrel says it is good for your back. He gets old-man back pain. He still asks about the diaries a lot. I wish he hadn't read them before giving them to me. But on the other hand, I'm glad because he now remembers what happened through my mother's teenage eyes as well as through his own and so feels guilty.

When Mum was alive, I thought of Joel as my best friend, but really it was probably my mum. But now she isn't here and that means Joel actually is my best friend and I want him to be safe and loved and happy. The power dynamic in his relationship could be off. I mean, it probably is. The older you are, the more money and experience you have and it's not fair.

I think I might hate Duncan. I wish I knew his surname so I could stalk him on the Internet. I probably could find it out if Joel hadn't blocked me on things. I also could probably find out through Ciara, but I don't know how comfortable Joel will be if I tell everyone his business. His ill-advised sugar-daddy business. They probably are doing it. He's that much older, I bet he would expect it. And Joel is so needy. He's wanted a boyfriend for ages upon ages. Now he has one, he would probably do a lot to keep him. Things he isn't ready for. Or feels he is. At least he can't get pregnant. He could catch things though. If he isn't using condoms.

Everyone but me has such grown-up concerns. My biggest thing is Joel being my friend again and being happy. The being happy is for me not him. I think he mostly is. At least I hope so. He deserves to be. I'm not sure that I do. I'm very selfish.

Joel I'm hearing things about you.

What things?

About you and an older man called Duncan. Should I be worried?

No. You only worry about your friends and we aren't friends any more.

I am still your friend.

Well, I'm not yours, so stay out of my business.

I want to respect your privacy. But I am worried. Do your parents know?

Is that a threat? This is typical you. Gah.

It is not typical me. I am being atypical. I promise. ☺

☹

So, I'm guessing they don't know then. Which is fine, but if they knew, they really wouldn't like it. And I'm not sure if being a good friend even though you aren't my friend any more means that I should tell them or not tell them.

It means you should not tell them. Duh.

I'm not convinced.

What would it take to convince you?

Tea and company.

That is blackmail.

Yes.

You are blackmailing me into hanging out with you.

Yes.

You are pathetic.

Yes, but you are worth it. ☺

Christ.

Free Friday evening? Should we meet at your house or mine, or somewhere neutral, like a coffee shop or the cinema?

Busy Friday.

Are you seeing Duncan, the grown-up man?

Don't call him that. Yes. I can meet you Saturday
in town. For an hour.

I'll take what I can get. ☺

I wish there was a hatredy face that I could send
you. The closest I can get is this. But, like, imagine
it times a hundred in terms of bile. 😈

Harsh. Still excited to see you, though. ☺

And I am. I am ridiculously excited to see my friend
whom I have blackmailed into spending time with me
through subtle threats that weren't very subtle. I can't
decide whether this makes me awesome or not. I am
looking forward to Saturday. I probably won't ask him
sex-questions till we've gone for hush-tea at least once
more. Hush-tea is like hush-money, only I get to spend
time with Joel and so it's better. I miss him so much. I
am such a loser.

I wonder what I'll wear? Karen dresses pretty well,
and I know it's not like a date, but I feel like I should
make sartorial choices that show that I bring just as
much, if not more, to the table. My eyeliner definitely
needs work. If this were a date with a normal boy, I
would ring Ciara and be all 'WHAT AM I GOING TO
WEAR?' and 'AGH'. Actually, if this were a date with a
normal boy I:

a.

Wouldn't ring Ciara to talk about clothes.

b.

Wouldn't hugely care what I wore. I mean, I would a bit, but Joel is more important. More important than anyone.

c.

I mean, we've been friends since pre-school. We went to Niamh's creche together, and both liked the fat crayons better than the skinny, and both fancied the same boy, Kevin (which is kind of fore-shadowy and creepy even though he didn't look like other Kevin at all, but more like Aladdin from the Disney cartoon. Aladdin or Prince Eric from *The Little Mermaid*. If they had a baby, it would have been Creche Kevin), because he had dark twisty hair and light-up runners and freckles the colour of caramel.

d.

Felix is a bit like how I imagine straight haired, grown-up Kevin would look. Only without the light-up runners, obviously.

e

I wish he liked me back.

f

I wish Joel loved me again.
The best-friend kind of love we used to share
where both of us were family together.

g

Sitting in the café beside Felix, I got a wave of jealousy
for Joel. I will never have a life exciting enough to
warrant interventions.

h

Would it be weird to bring a series of helpful and
informative sex-pamphlets to the café?

i

Because you can get an STD from very little sexual contact
if you are unlucky, and it's best to be careful.

j.

I'd hate to get an STD — you'd feel all filthy.

K.

And not in a good way.

l.

Good-filthy is a nice feeling.

m.

But Kevin-shaped experience has taught me it is all too often followed by bad-filthy.

n.

I wonder if Kevin ever felt bad-filthy after we hooked up?

O.

It can't be just a girl thing. The shame of letting yourself be taken for granted.

P.

He was the granted-taker, though, so was probably fine.

q.

If Duncan ever takes Joel for granted I will
scratch his aging eyes out.

r.

There is so much I don't know about how people interact
romantically. I wish I had a boyfriend.

s.

But then I would worry so much about keeping him
and acting around him and whether or not he was
interesting enough and whether or not I was.
It would be pretty bothersome.

t.

Maybe boarding-school Robb could be my summer boy.
I mean, I don't exactly fancy him that much, but it would
be a welcome distraction from not being a very good person.

u.

And also, it might make me feel prettier.

V.

I don't feel very pretty at the moment.

W.

Not that being pretty is the be all and end all.

X.

But if you don't feel like you are a very good person, feeling attractive on the outside couldn't hurt.

Y.

I am so looking forward to Saturday.

Z.

I wonder how Joel will be.

If he will hate me.

AA.

He totally will.

A A comes after **Z** in lists, a right-back-to-the-beginning that ties in with all of my problems. I have to work on being a better person than I am. But I am not going to do that by Saturday so the best I can do is have gossip.

I texted Robb with two bees to meet up. I hate that Kevin cancelled our ice-cream because he has a girl-friend. It reeks of 'I only want to be friends with you if there is hooking up as well as friendship'. And that is not OK. Although, that is kind of how I feel about Robb with two bees. Because he is not a very interesting boy, but he is quite cute and I could see myself enjoying kissing him, if only to stop him from talking. And show Kevin that he doesn't matter. And show Joel that I have inter-esting things happen that he doesn't know about. And to show Felix that other boys fancy me, that I am someone who it is possible to find attractive. Not that it will make a difference now, but it could stew like a tea-bag and result in

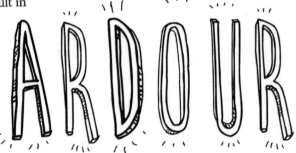

at some point.

Isn't 'ardour' a lovely word? You never really hear it used, outside of a romance novel.

I am reading a book about a Viking who is a lot more supportive than Fintan. Is it too much to expect that the father of your child be as supportive as a storybook Viking? If not more-so? Though it would be tough to be more supportive than Godric the Bold. He had the local wise woman make balm for the tired feet of his lady-love and everything. My feet are also tired. And yet, I remain balm-less.

I finally ran out of romance novels left behind by Mum last Christmas so I have been tracking down ones of a similar nature (knights, Vikings, sexy time travel) in charity shops for the past while. I wish that I could travel through time. Apart from the obvious, saving Mum from stupid drunken drivers, I could get up to all sorts of mischief with hilarious consequences. Romance-novel time travel doesn't work like time-machine time travel, though.

It's a little different. You don't have control over where you get sent. It's either a mystical love wind, or the curse of a spurned warlock, or those meddling faerie folk that send you wherever, and initially you're all, 'AGH!' and 'How will a hard-nosed career woman (albeit with a tragic back-story and secret mushy centre) like me be able to cope in a medieval keep? They don't have electric showers or anything.' But it works out in the end, because you adapt and the handsome warlord who distrusted you initially comes to fall in love with you and then you do kissing and things in an apiary or a solar or somewhere else that is quintessentially of its time. And then something happens to tear you apart, but it all gets sorted. And while that would be fun, I'd really rather have a mum and still be friends with Joel than know

A
LOVE
STRONGER
THAN
TIME
ITSELF,

thank you very much.

I wonder if there's anything I could do to make Fintan more excited about the baby.

need, like, a love-potion. But for friendship. Ciara thinks I am in the wrong for blackmailing Joel.

'It just seems so needy, Prim. Make him chase you.'

'He is a friend, not a boy.'

'Nevertheless.'

She does not take her own advice, this Ciara, she is constantly texting me, wanting to hang out and things. Which I love, because she is my good friend. But when we started being friends, she was *always* texting. And it's not like there is another solution to the Joel problem. I mean, I could just wait him out and keep on intermittently apologising, but that hasn't been working so far and I really want to see him.

Ciara actually had an ulterior motive in calling around today. She wants me to go with her to the family planning clinic so she can start planning her family. Her current plan is for it not to happen for at least a decade and a bit. But things with Syzmon have been heating up a little. She's mainly worried about pregnancy, because they're both virgins and you can't catch STDs from being a virgin. Being a virgin is, like, the opposite of how you catch STDs. You can get HIV if you're one, from blood transfusions gone wrong and other things. But you'd be hard pressed to get chlamydia. When I think about things like chlamydia, I feel confident in the fact that I'm (probably) definitely not ready to have sex yet. But even if you're never going to take a ride on the marital love train, as Grandma Lily liked to call it, it is best to be informed about these things, so you can give advice to passing Ciaras.

'Not that things with Syzmon weren't hot before,' she said, flicking her hair as if daring me to judge her. 'But I keep getting caught up in stuff and almost going all the way.'

'How can you do that accidentally?'

'Stuff gets rubbed against other stuff and things start to seem like good ideas and possibly needs. It's all very passionate and so on and so forth, but I had intended waiting until things were nice and legal until we did THE DEED.' She widens her eyes when she says 'THE DEED', emphasising it's deedy importance.

'You mean wait for marriage?'

'No. Until my seventeenth birthday. Or shortly afterwards.'

'Cool. That makes sense. Do you, like, feel ready and stuff?'

Ciara looked out the window, at the garden. There were bees but no birds, which may have been an omen but probably wasn't. (The bees love our lavender plant.) 'How do you know if you feel ready? I mean, I totally want to sometimes, but other times I'm, like, "WHAT IF I GOT PREGNANT?" and "AAAGGH". It would totally ruin my plans to go to millinery school.'

'Babies are wont to do that. It is a tough one. Do you know what sort of contraception you want?'

'Well, I kind of want to get the pill, but I can't ask Mam's GP for it, because they are, like, friends and stuff, so it would totally get back to her, which is why it would be better to go to the family planning clinic and get it from someone who is a doctor who doesn't still try to give me lollipops and stickers when I visit. Also, I am **NOT** buying condoms.'

She said this as if buying condoms were up there with selling heroin.

I offered to buy them for her, which was actually pretty generous of me, because I'd get a bit nervous about that sort of thing too. I don't even like buying tampons.

'Would you? Wow!' she said. 'I don't know, though. Isn't buying condoms a bit of a *slutty* thing to do?'

'What? No! Why would you think that?'

'Well, you have to buy, like, this big box of them. I mean, I think you can get, like, little packs of three, but that's still committing to have sex three times, which is huge. I mean, I'm not even sure I want to once, you know?'

'Buying condoms does not mean you have to use them, Ciara.'

'But they'd only go to waste otherwise.'

'Condoms are **NOT** ham sandwiches. They don't like "go off" or anything if you don't use them within six weeks.'

'I think buying them is the boy's job.' She nodded her head, the way she sometimes does when she agrees with herself. 'Only ... I don't want to ask Syzmon to buy them, because I don't want him getting any ideas. I want it to be a lovely surprise if I decide to share my body with him.'

Ciara actually says stuff like

'SHARE MY BODY WITH HIM'.

I lent her some of Mum's Viking books a couple of years ago and they really took.

'I wonder if Joel is sharing his body with that Duncan creep?' I tried not to sound like I was making air quotes with my voice when I said 'sharing his body'. It was really challenging.

'You are **NOT** to ask him that on Saturday.'

'Why not?'

'Because it is private, and you need to woo him back with niceness and not being judgey before he is your friend-you-can-say-anything-to again.'

This is sound advice, but I am not sure if I will be able to follow it. I can't believe Ciara is thinking about having sex when I don't even have a boyfriend. It's so unfair.

Not that I want to lose my virginity, but I would like to have the option, in the context of a loving relationship, of course. I'll most likely end up losing it to Kevin (or someone just as bad) on a pile of coats, while she gets roses and scented candles and a soft and tender playlist she is probably already in the process of compiling.

Mum didn't lose it to Fintan. Which is why reading your mum's old diaries is a mix of

&

.

She had a secondary-school boyfriend, who she was with for the first six months of college. His name was Seán, which is a very normal name for a man to have. She broke up with him for not being THE ONE. She has this whole bit about wishing she had met him when she was twenty-five or thirty and ready to get married and all that. She was weirdly sure she was going to get married. It is kind of sad she never met anyone she liked enough, apart from Fintan for an ill-advised period pre-and-post-me.

Sometimes I wish I had stayed with Seán.

I wouldn't be happy, but I wouldn't be pregnant either.

Probably.

Mum loved me once I came out. I know this for a fact because she has written about it. But I'm kind of hurt by the fact that she wasn't happy about the possibility of a me for a long time. She didn't want a baby. She didn't want to stop being irresponsible and she didn't want to have to worry about a whole other person. She was weirdly OK with the idea of being forever tied to Fintan, until he messed things up. I still don't one hundred per cent get why she wanted to be with him so badly. He is not that cool. Nor is he that handsome. Unless you're into enormous noses and facial topiary. And he was so much older. Perhaps Joel could shed some light on the fancying-older-men thing when I meet up with him.

I miss my mum, always will, but I don't think I realised how complex she was until I started reading her diaries. Three and a half years after she died. You think I would have copped on to it earlier. I mean, she was a mum, she was *my* mum, but she was also a person with intricacies and worries and feelings about things that were grey and blue and green, not black and white. She was as much of a person as I am now. Which is hard to get my head around.

I feel bad that I didn't appreciate her enough. But I was a kid when she died – I mean, I'm still a kid now, more or less. But I was a proper child then. I didn't know. It isn't that I didn't care. I didn't know how hard it was for her. She loved me, but she raised me on her own, for the most part. And babies are very high-maintenance. Like needy fiancées, but more so.

I read the things she wrote, the who she was, the fragments of her self over and over again. Balancing accounts. Lashing interpretations on top of them, as though they were *The Merchant of Venice*, or *To Kill a Mockingbird*, or any other text I had to study. I don't know why I feel compelled to do that. It's not like anything will bring her back.

But I do want her to come back because I could be a better daughter now. I wouldn't be as selfish. I'd help more in the house, listen when she needed me to listen. I feel like she put all this work into me, and now when it's about to pay off, when I'm mature enough to be a proper friend as well as daughter, she's gone. And Dad is here to reap the benefits of the way she raised me. It isn't fair on her (or me). But I still keep reading, because maybe something's hidden in the text. An Easter egg. A clue. A recipe for strange important somethings.

I really think the baby will be a boy.

I keep wanting steak and potatoes.

Hearty, manly things.

I met Robb with two bees again today. He looked me up and down when I walked up to him outside Easons on O'Connell Street and said, 'You're looking well.' I don't know why, but the way he said it kind of put my back up. Like he was objectifying me, but not in a nice way. I can't really put my finger on why it niggled but it did. He wouldn't have said that to a boy. And it made me think about all the times he hadn't said that to me and wonder if I wasn't looking well before.

Maybe I was edgy because I was going to be meeting Joel later, after Robb, for blackmail-tea-and-catch-up. Robb with two bees will never be as good as Joel. It was nice to ramble around town with him, though (Robb I mean), chatting about films and music and books and TV shows. Nice neutral topics of conversation. He gets a bit superior about things. Like, he assumes that he will know more than me on any given subject. Which is nonsense, because he thought Bolivia was in eastern Europe. I do not know much about Bolivia, but I do know what continent it is in.

AND ROBB WITH TWO BEES DID NOT.

Quote from Prim's mum's diary

'It kind of sounds eastern European, though,' he said, doing a ridiculous approximation of a Russian accent:

'I see what you mean. But it is in South America.'
'Are you sure?'
'Yes.'
And then he googled it, hoping to prove me wrong.

Oh, Robb with two bees!

I don't mean to make him sound completely dreadful, though. Because he isn't. It's just that I do not think that our destiny is written in the stars. I'm also fairly sure he thinks I fancy him. Well, I mean, I do keep meeting up with him and messaging him and things. But that is ONLY because I am lonely and bored.

I didn't tell Joel that, though, when we met afterwards. From the way I went on to Joel about him, you'd swear Robb was my new bestie. It was so good to see my real (former? current?) bestie again. He didn't hug me. I kind of knew he wouldn't, but I really wanted to hug him, to hold him close and tell him he was awesome and I'd missed him.

I have to admit I had met Robb (kind of) so me and Joel would have something neutrally gossipy to talk about. Is that terrible? It kind of is, isn't it? It totally is. I kind of wanted to be all: 'I have a life, even when you are not around to be my social crutch' and 'I have made a new friend who is a boy' and 'I have people interested in me too, like you have the mysterious and possibly dodgy Duncan.'

Because my life is not very interesting and Joel makes it more interesting when he is in it, because he is awesome and always up for devilment and doing things, while I kind of prefer to stay in my bubble of friends and stuff. Also Joel has way more friends than I do. I mean he is not short of companionship. I have Ciara. And Ella. That is the extent of my inner circle. I mean, I'd love to include Felix in there, because he is a big ride and I'd like him to be my friend with or without benefits. But we aren't that close. I mean, I'd never ring Felix crying or for a random chat about dachshunds or whatever. So basically my inner circle is an inner triangle. An inner square if you count Joel.

I was trying to make Joel jealous with all my talk of Robb. I do not know if I succeeded. He made me jealous with all his talk of Duncan. Nary an anecdote went by that didn't involve the aging pervert. They met one night when he was out with Karen. He pointedly mentioned Karen a few times while we were making the awkward small-talk leading up to me glutting my feelings all over him. I think it is really hypocritical that he was now hanging out with someone who has called our friend Ella a retard on more than one occasion and wouldn't hang out with me, even though I didn't even use hate-speech when I outed her, just said that she was 'a mean lesbian or possibly a mean bisexual woman'.

'So you and Karen are, like, total besties now?' I said.

'Don't use that sarcastic tone with me, Prim. I don't even want to be here. Karen is worth ten of you.'

'No she isn't.'

'She is mean. But also really fun, so it kind of balances out.' He emphasised the word 'fun' as though it were delicious and alien. Which is nonsense because I am total fun. Like off-the-chain fun-levels right here all day everyday. I can't believe he tried to imply he didn't have fun with me. We had mild-to-moderate fun on a number of occasions. Sometimes we dialled it right up to severe. This normally involved move-busting or gluing things on children. I wonder what kind of fun he had with Karen. I bet it was mean, immoral, reprehensible fun. The kind of fun you have on a road-trip with human trafficking.

'Do you miss me even a little bit?' I asked him.

'I do. But I can't be friends with someone who doesn't respect people's right to be themselves.' He stirred sugar into his tea. Round and round and round it went. Clink and clink and clink. I felt a tirade building up inside me because I am not a bad person. I'm just not. I made a mistake and people do that all the bloody time. They make mistakes and then they get forgiven. Look at Dad. Before I knew it my mouth was open and all the feelings were just pouring out, surprising both of us.

'But who she is is hateful, Joel. She opens her mouth and all this bile spews out and it is hurtful. She said my mum got SQUISHED.

SQUISHED.

That was not OK. And I feel that you hanging out with her and picking her over me is so *unfair* or something.' I may have started to cry at this point. The spoon inside the teacup had stopped moving. Joel's voice got deeper, softer. The way it does when he is being sad or gentle with me. When he is trying to ease the answers out.

'When did she say that thing about your mum?'

'At the dancey thing last year. Remember I went home early because she told me about Mac?'

'Yeah.'

'So her *exact words* were, "His dad squished your mum." That's not OK. You loved my mum and it's not OK that you are hanging out with someone who disrespected her memory like that. And it's not OK that you are being so mean to me when you know I have always loved and accepted you and –'

'But –'

'Let me finish.' I was kind of full-on purple and quivery with woe at this point. In a café. In the middle of town.

GLAM.

'And I thought I wanted you to be my friend again. I thought I was in the wrong. But the more I analyse it, Joel, the more it seems like you were looking for a reason to friend-break-up with me, because Karen has basically been bullying me since first year, or trying to anyway. And you picked her over me because I did *one* mean thing.'

'You also punched her in the face that time.'

'She called Ella a retard, Joel.'

'Oh yeah. She did. Jesus. I'd forgotten.'

'Ella hasn't. And I haven't. And I think that you not talking to me was way more about the Kevin thing than it was about the Karen thing. And I am sorry, because he was horrible to me as well, in a different way, and you are more important than he is and I shouldn't have done that to you when I knew you fancied him. It's just ... I hardly have all the boys running after me. I mean, I'm not gorgeous like Ciara or skinny-quirky-pretty like Ella. I kind of have to take what I can get.'

'You shouldn't have kissed him,' Joel said, and his face was tight. He ripped open a sugar packet and spilled the contents on the table.

'I know.'

'And then kept on kissing him.' He was making a little mountain out of the sugar, then smoothing it down, spreading it thin.

'I know.' I looked at the granules on the table. I wanted to wipe them away, to tidy them up. My hands were in my lap. I kept them there. Joel sighed.

'You know you aren't, like, ugly or anything. I mean, you've got great hair and you're fun to be around and you didn't inherit Fintan's nose. Any boy would be lucky to be with you.'

'No they wouldn't. I'm a mess. I mean, look at all this. I was going to be cool and woo you back with tales of my fascinating life without you.'

I tried to flick my hair. It didn't work. But Joel's interest was evidently piqued because he made suggestive eye contact.

'Fascinating, eh?'

'Honestly, it's been crap. You're kind of my favourite person.' We were quiet for a while, letting the truth of that sink in. The weight of it.

'You never told me Karen said that thing. You bottle things up too much.'

'Maybe you are right.'

He is right. I amn't going to change my ways or anything but he is right. I bottle and explode in carefully managed situations by myself. I hate the thought of casualties. Or causing grief. Collateral damage in my war to not be crap. That kind of thing.

We paused and he mumbled something.

'Wait. What?'

'I'm sorry, Prim. I'm really, really sorry. I should have asked you about things. I should have been there for Roderick's funeral. I mean, I'd known him since he was a baby.'

'That *was* pretty harsh of you. We buried him with Mum. For my birthday party.'

'I know you did. Ciara told me all about it. I asked her things about you. Well, not so much with asking. She tends to talk about you pretty freely.' This was true. I nodded.

'Sometimes I think she's basically my no-sex wife,' I said.

'I'm not going to even bother unpacking that. Can we be friends again?'

'Only if you tell me about your ridiculous older-gent sex-pervert of a boyfriend.'

Joel shook his head, but also kept on talking. 'He is only three out of those four things.'

'Which three?'

'That would be telling.'

And then we spoke of Duncan once again.

Duncan has dirty blond hair and enjoys surfing. They met at a house party, where Karen abandoned Joel to go find drugs. Duncan shared his beer with Joel and made sure he was included in the conversation. Duncan is kind like that. He fought against asking Joel out for ages, because he was worried Joel was too young. He is a very moral and upstanding dater of children.

'I'm finished my Junior Cert, Prim. And it isn't like that. Don't make me stop talking to you again.'

'I can't not mock you about being a boy-toy, Joely. My tongue would spasm from the wanting to and then dry out and curl up from frustration in my mouth. I might die.'

'You are not going to die, Prim.'

'Of course I'm going to die, Joel. Everybody is.'

'You're so morbid.'

I triangled my hands, like a good Caroline. 'I blame the cognitive behavioural therapy.'

'How is that going, by the way?'

Joel has always been very interested in therapy. He once told me that when he came out, he was secretly hoping that his parents would pay for him to go. They ended up accepting him instead. Which is probably better.

'Mostly OK. But it can be hard.'

'How so?'

I knew from the head on Joel that he wanted me to talk about the cutting. But I wasn't going to. It's not con-versation-fodder. I barely even acknowledge it to Caroline. Joel knows because of conjecture and seeing my scars in passing, when I'd be changing into my pyjamas or whatever. Since he's come out as gay, both our parents have been laxer about the whole being in each other's bedrooms for long periods of time thing.

'Just things. Saying things out loud. I bet they'd send you to therapy if you told them about Duncan.'

Joel nodded slowly. 'You're probably right. But then I wouldn't get to see Duncan. He has a gauged piercing and a tattoo of a pigeon on his calf. Dad would hate him.'

'So would Fintan, by the sounds of it. Maybe I should date him too.'

Joel laughed. I hadn't made Joel laugh in

quite a while and it felt lovely. 'You can't have this one. He is a proper gay man.'

'Sexuality is fluid, Joel. And I can look pretty manly in the right light. Have you guys done the deed?'

'Prim!'

'Joel! What? I'm curious.'

'He wants to wait until I'm seventeen.' Joel fiddled with another sugar packet, but didn't open it. I approved of Duncan's self-control by picking at my nail polish awkwardly.

'How chivalrous of him! He clearly is a proper gent.'

'I think so. Ooh! Actually I forgot to ask what the story was with your dad and Sorrel. Mam saw them hanging out like a pair of chums in town.'

'They're getting on quite well. She does some minding of me and some cleaning of our house in exchange for money. Freelance acupuncture and Reiki aren't going too well at the moment.'

'I hope I'm not poor when I'm older.'

'Me too. I mean, I don't want to be Fintan-rich. But I'd like to have enough money not to have to do cleaning on the side. Not that she cleans very well. I have to follow her around with the cloth. Dad mostly likes her for the chats. She's kind of his therapist.'

Joel put his head dramatically between his hands. 'Everyone has a therapist but me.'

'Liam doesn't.' Liam is Joel's father. He is an extremely confident man who coaches hurling.

'Liam has never had a moment of self-doubt in his life. Even when he found out he'd raised a gay man.'

'You are not a man yet, Joel.'

'I am. I am a young adult.'

'I don't know. I'm the same age as you, and I don't feel very adult at all.'

'What makes you an adult? I wonder.'

'Voting. Or doing it.'

'But not at the same time.'

Even though we clicked into our old friendship like there hadn't been a few months in the middle where he'd cut me out, I'm wary. Because he might start hating me again and never stop and then I would be lonely. It is important to carve out friendships with new, less-prone-to-hate-me people for this reason.

Fintan has asked me to marry him. I've said yes, because I love him and I want my parents not to be angry with me. The latter is not a very grown-up reason to get married, but I think the former is pretty solid. Also there is wanting my child to have a traditional two-parent family. I mean, that's the ideal, isn't it?

I called over to Ella's for tea today. She prefers to stay in than go out, although she has her moments. We watched a documentary about a lion cub who was raised in 1960s London, and then got big, so his owners decided to send him back to Africa to live with other lions, so he could be happy and fulfilled and not a public menace. There was a bit at the end, where the lion was all hanging out with his new pack and his old owners visited and he recognised them and went over to them and gave them a big excited yet gentle lion hug. It made me properly sob. Unexpected reunions always do that to

Quote from Prim's mum's diary

me. In films and books anyway. I don't think I've ever had one in real life, unless making up with Joel counts. Ella rubbed my shoulder awkwardly. She's not too gone on hugs. Felix came in midway through my sobathon.

'You must be at the bit where they visit him in Africa.'

I nodded.

'I'm pausing it until she stops crying,' said Ella, rubbing my shoulder all the while.

'Good plan. It might be a while, though. That was a pretty moving scene.'

'Felix cried as well,' said Ella, who was going to rub a hole through the fabric of my T-shirt if she wasn't careful. 'Not as much as you, though. You're pretty sad.'

'I'm not sad.'

'Yes, you are, you're crying.'

'I suppose I am.'

Felix came back in with a box of tissues and eventually I quieted down enough to watch the rest of it with Ella. Then we went to her room and played with Mr Cat for a while.

'I wonder if Mr Cat would give you a glorious lion hug if he were a lion instead of a cat and you had returned him to Africa so he could socialise with other magnificent lions?'

'He would if I had cheese.' Ella knows Mr Cat pretty well.

'He probably would anyway. He's pretty loyal to you.'

Mr Cat rubs and cuddles up to Ella as though his name were Mr Dog. With everyone else, he acts like a normal cat who could not give a toss about you unless there was something in it for him. Like cheese or catnip or a stick with a feather on the end for him to hunt. Sticks with feathers on the end of them are endlessly fascinating to Mr Cat, so long as they're in motion. If they are perfectly still, there is no sport in hunting them and he could not care less. Kind of like Kevin with me. I got a text from him last night asking who this Robb fella was. As if he cared.

'He probably does care a bit,' said Ella.

'Not enough to want to be my boyfriend.'

'He can't be your boyfriend when he already has a girlfriend.'

'I know, duh. But I wish he had picked me instead of Siobhán. I wonder why he texted.'

Ella thought about it. 'Because he mightn't want you, but he doesn't want anyone else to have you either?'

'That's not very nice of him.'

'Boys are not very nice people. Caleb is kissing other girls now.'

This was interesting. 'Oh?'

'He keeps texting me about it. I think he is trying to make me jealous so I will get back together with him.'

'That would probably work on me.'

'Felix said the same thing. He is quite needy.'

Me too, Felix. Look at all we have in common. Let's have twenty babies and a cocker spaniel called Oscar that we dress in little jumpers.

'And would you think about getting back together with Caleb?'

'No. I like him a lot, but I don't fancy him enough to be his girlfriend any more.'

'Makes sense. I wonder why people stop fancying other people.'

This is a pretty big question for me. Not only would it solve the mystery of Mum and Dad's weirdly twisty little romance thing but it would provide me with much needed Kevin-closure.

'They get used to them, and then they are not as interesting.'

This was not the answer I was expecting, but it made a lot of sense. Ella is really wise. We made pizza for dinner, with a side salad. Ella put raisins in the salad and I thought it was going to taste weird, but it was actually pretty epic. I think I would like going over to her house even if I didn't fancy her brother a ridiculous amount. We could hear him playing his bass guitar through the walls. He is in two bands. The Deep Tinkers (who do a sort of trad-rock fusion thing and often play at alcohol-free events for Dublin Youth) and Promises, Promises, which is his 'commercial venture' and plays covers at weddings. The members of both bands are exactly the same, but they didn't want to sully the Tinker name with Abba medleys and power ballads.

There is something really attractive about playing an instrument. It might explain why Mum fell so hard for Dad. He can play the guitar, the bass guitar, the piano and a bit of the zither. I used to think this was really cool when I was little and he would pick out the songs I liked on his keyboard to impress me when I only saw him at weekends. Mum was never overly enthusiastic when I told her how cool that was. She never really moaned about Dad in front of me, but sometimes I overheard her grumbling to her friends. We tended to live in small places. I have way more privacy in this house now. Which is a good thing, because I am a teenager and don't enjoy being too observable. Not because I do too many secret things, but because I want to be my own person and have stuff that's just mine.

Roderick was a thing that was just mine. No-one else I knew had a rat. And he was so cute and friendly and clever. My small bestie. Ella understands how important animals are. Ciara not so much. I think she has them down as less than family and boyfriends, but slightly more than an accessory you quite like. Whereas for me, Roderick was on an even enough keel with Fintan. But he was a damn sight more important than stupid Kevin. I kind of miss stupid Kevin, though. He had broad shoulders and a warm neck. And a ridiculous little dog called Wayne Rooney. As boys who fancied me went, he was pretty much the only one. I hope I meet another one before I die. Preferably before the summer is over. Ella thinks I will, but she's not so sure about herself.

'People think I've got an intellectual disability just because I'm on the spectrum.'

'But you get better results than most people.'

'I know, right? Some of Mam's friends speak to me really, really slowly. As though I were a cat to be coaxed out of trees.'

'That sucks.'

'Yeah. I don't like it at all. People say that we can't pick up on social cues, but it's very easy to know when you're being patronised.'

'Blerg.'

'I know. I think that even if I did have an intellectual disability, I would not want to be spoken to like that. There are an awful lot of things I want from a boyfriend, and being talked down to is not one of them. So it's not that I don't think I can get a boyfriend, it's just that I want someone who is properly special.'

I nodded, thinking about her lovely brother with his smile and shoulders. 'Me too.'

'Prim,' said Ella, maintaining excellent eye-contact, 'are you thinking about Felix?'

'**NO**.' I looked away.

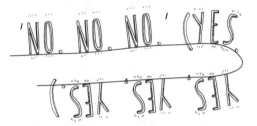

'Then why are you blushing?'
'I'm not.'

'You totally are. Blushing is a social cue. I have been trained to notice these things.'

Ella sometimes goes to social-skills classes to learn how to read people. She treats it like a science and could probably be a world-class poker-player if she had any interest in cards at all. Sometimes I wish I could go to social-skills class. It sounds dossier than therapy and if I were more clued in to how to behave around people maybe I could briefly trick Felix into thinking I was cool.

Sorrel picked me up from Ella's and drove me home. She was ostensibly over to do some ironing (Dad hates ironing), but Dad ended up talking to her for ages as she

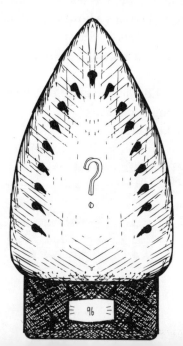

tended to his house. Dad doesn't think that cleaning is woman's work exactly, but he certainly has no trouble employing women to do it for him. Mum was worried, when she was engaged to Dad, about what being a wife would mean. If she would have to change her life to suit Fintan's. (The answer to this was yes.)

Hedda broke up with Dad because she didn't want to marry him and he wanted to marry her. This is apparently a reason that grown-ups have for breaking up. Teenagers don't have to worry about wanting to marry their boy- or girlfriends. Because it is a truth universally acknowledged that teenage weddings are creepy. It **WOULD** have been creepy if Dad had actually gone through with marrying Mum. He didn't call off the wedding because of creepiness. But it must have been on his mind.

It wasn't really on hers. She was more focused on the growing-a-human-being-inside-of-her aspect of the whole affair. And also whether or not he was cheating on her the whole time they were together. Awkward questions tend to make Dad flail around a bit and then buy me things. Unless he's grumpy, in which case he just snaps at you and turns up the telly.

Dad's been watching a lot of historical documentaries recently. Maybe because he is old. My father is an old, old dude. An old, old dude who liked young, young women once upon a time. I suppose he still kind of does. It's just that now they're young compared to him as opposed to fresh out of secondary school and ripe for corruption and impregnation.

We've booked a wedding band! This is really happening! My parents are not necessarily delighted, but their relief has been translated into something approaching delight and that will do for now.

I have decided to be excited about this.

I need something to be excited about.

The baby isn't cutting it, as yet.

aroline is stupid. She keeps listening to me. I'm supposed to find this soothing or something, I think. She then usually asks a question with no question mark to it, like, 'Tell me about school,' and then just waits and I hate pauses and, I mean, she's nice even though she's stupid and I like to please people so I fill the spaces in the air with all these words but they don't necessarily mean all that much, if you get me. Sometimes I sigh and look at my hands.

I told her about making up with Joel and she didn't even say how great it was. She smiled at me and nodded her head, like, 'Tell me more.' I can't believe it is properly a job to get all up in people's business and have them pay you for it. It seems more like a cruel trick. Not that Caroline is cruel. I mean, she does interact with me sometimes and it's not like I don't like the sound of my own voice, it's just in the room alone with her, listening to myself, I sound different. Sort of broken. Sort of off. And that is the last thing that I want to seem to people and normally I don't think that I do. Seem that way, I mean.

Caroline is dearer than Triona, my old therapist, was. Evidently, Dad decided to bust out the platinum card when it came to me actually self-harming as opposed to just being sad for a very good reason, like when I went to Triona for bereavement counselling. Triona was dreadful. Caroline is miles better than she is. She helps me come up with plans to make things better. Like I keep a ball of string beside my bed now, and when I want to cut I make a cat's cradle instead and then my hands are too tangled and busy to get up to any devilment. Cat's cradles are very innocent things. Real childhoody. I miss being a kid. Instead of a 'young lady'.

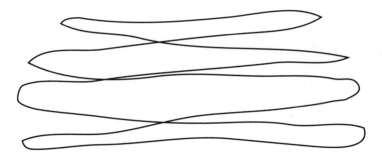

Nineteen is way more grown-up-sounding than eighteen. So I'm glad my birthday comes before the baby. Also, a baby is quite a grown-up thing to have. I mean, you can't have a baby and not be a woman. I wish I were older. I can't quite get my head around being someone's wife. Or someone's mum. Jesus Christ.

I am really trying to stop swearing. When the baby comes, he or she will not benefit from a sweary mother. Whoops a daisy. Fairy-cakes. Mother of pearl. These are functional alternatives, I think. I hope. Christ on a bike is Dad's favourite exclamation. That and Jesus Wept.

I am going to take up crochet. I think. It will be something else to do with my hands when I get fidgety. My cat's cradle string keeps tangling in a frustrating manner and I think it might be full of germs at this stage. No-one told me how often to change my string of not-slicing. And it's not the kind of question I can ask in therapy without Caroline worrying my mind scabs with her tongue. I don't need any more scars on my legs or stomach. I only have, like, five, but I don't need any more. They're kind of purple. I think that they would have faded better if I wasn't such a ridiculous scab-picker. I wonder, when I have a proper, sexy-times boyfriend, if he'll ask me what they are. Will I tell him the truth, remind him what his business is, or lie?

Lies about self-harm scars that I could tell my future Boyfriend

1.

I was mugged by a tiny person. Possibly a vicious child. They had a blade and slashed at me a few times when I wouldn't give them my phone. It was pretty hardcore.

2.

I fell foul of a particularly savage feral cat. One-eyed Tom was his name and he sliced at me with his magnificent claws one cold November Eve as I was perambulating about the town. I still hear tell of One-eyed Tom sometimes, and bear him no ill-will. Were he a man, I would probably have fallen for him.

3.

I cut myself shaving. My legs and stomach. I had a weirdly hairy stomach a while back but it isn't hairy any more because I've had extensive electrolysis on it.
Dad paid for it after I cut myself shaving.

4.

These are stretch marks from the secret baby I had, once upon a time. *stares into distance in a wistful manner*
(This one raises more questions than it answers, but I think it might work, because what kind of demented individual would lie about a secret baby? THIS ONE RIGHT HERE, YO. I also need to work on being less enthusiastically shouty, because my future boyfriend might not like the near-constant deafening that is part and parcel of this sexy little package. I also need to become a sexy little package. Maybe I should join a gym.)

Crochet involves hooks and wool and you can make small animals out of the wool by using the hook. This is called amigurumi, and I think I might make an amigurumi life-cycle of Roderick. A kind of IN MEMORIAM-type-dealy. A small rat, like he was when I first got him, then a gawky adolescent rat, then a splendid fellow that I could dress up in top-hats and things and, finally, an aging fogey who weighed almost nothing because his muscles were wasting away.

Isn't it odd that a marvellous way to remember my rat would be a REALLY creepy way to remember my mum? I look at photographs of her a lot. At different ages. I worry, though, that that could be quite dangerous. That when I'm remembering a thing, there'll all of a sudden be a photograph super-imposed on her face. I want to remember her in motion. A human, not an image.

I thought about getting Roderick taxidermied way back before he got sick, but Fintan was very against the idea. He hates stuffed animals. He once took me to the natural history museum, and after a while he had to let me wander around alone while he went for a reviving cup of coffee. My father is a very strange man. Who should have been nicer to my back-in-the-day mother. But you can't change the past. If I could, I'd be a busy girl, always erasing past mistakes. Like Kevin. Who is still with Siobhán.

Ciara says that Leona said that Siobhán said that she is in love with Kevin. Good luck to her. I am not in love with Kevin, but I do feel a certain ownership of him, seeing as how I had him first and everything. Robb with two bees is not the same as Kevin. Wouldn't it be weird if Kevin started spelling his name with two vees, just to be cool like an absolute prat? Kevvin, like? I wish he would. And I could be Primm and Joel could be Joell. Joell is a bit too close to the girl's name Joelle, though. Don't think he'd be too into that.

I'm not very pro-God at the moment.

Seeing as how he saw fit to have Fintan knock me up.

We'll get married in a church, though.

Because that's what's done.

Whoops a mother of pearling daisy.

R obb with two bees wants to go to the cinema with me. I think this might mean that kissing will happen. Cinemas are great places to do first kisses because it's dark and if the kissing doesn't work out no-one will see you and there will be a movie to watch and talk about afterwards, while you wait for your lift home. I have never kissed a boy with two bees before. Kevin didn't even have one bee. Also Robb is objectively pretty hot. He has a mean face, but in a handsome way. His bottom lip is really full, so it looks like he has a permanent case of the sulks. His bottom lip is a big pillowy part of the reason that I want to kiss him even though I don't fancy him. I don't think I do want to kiss him, but if he kissed me I would probably do some kissing back. I wonder what that would be like. I've only ever kissed Kevin and this random guy called Barry at a party Syzmon had.

Quote from Prim's mum's diary

Kevin was a better kisser than Barry. Oh, wait! There's Joel as well, who was probably my worst kiss because it wasn't expected or consensual. I don't really count it as my actual first kiss. He was only doing it to prove to this guy Liam that he wasn't gay or something. It was more of a lip-mash than a kiss. And afterwards, we had this massive bust-up and he told me I kissed 'like a bullfrog' and, sometimes, when I kiss a boy I wonder if I am doing anything bullfroggy. I do have quite a wide mouth, like a frog. But I'm not, like, catching flies with my tongue or anything like that. And what did Joel even mean? I mean it's not like he has any vast experience with frenching bullfrogs.

Isn't 'frenching' a weird term? It comes up in books about old-timey high-school and I'm kind of wondering if I should bring it back, because shifting isn't the nicest term there is. It kind of sounds like something you'd do to a reluctant cow. I normally say 'making out', which is another Americanism, but it covers a multitude and sometimes you do want to make it clear that only kissing was involved in a given situation. Same goes for 'hooking up'. Because sometimes that means sex, and you could really hurt someone's feelings by going around the place implying that you had had sex with them when you really hadn't. Frenching is peculiar said out loud but I think I could get Ciara on board with it. She's very into old-lady-isms because of Grandma Lily.

I have asked Joel about the bullfrog thing a few times, and he said he was only saying it to hurt me, but the things that are the best at hurting people are the things that are kind of sort of true as well as mean and I worry that it was one of those ones. I don't want to kiss like a bullfrog. I want to kiss like someone who is good at kissing. And I definitely want to be better at kissing than stupid Karen, who has shifted about fifty boys and that's before she turned into a lesbian. Maybe she is only a lesbian because she shifted all the boys in Ireland and now there are no boys left and it was either switch to women or emigrate. That was a pretty homophobic comment. I'd never make a comment like that about Joel or even about Duncan, the adult lover of young boys. I'm only a bigot when it comes to Karen and that is because she deserves it. I can't imagine wanting to kiss her on her stupid evil face and am very nonplussed as to why she gets more action than me when my face is clever and not evil. She is prettier than I am, though. And Good at Make-Up. I would like to be Good at Make-Up. I'd blame it on my mum not being around any more, but she wasn't too gone on make-up and I doubt she would have schooled me in the womanly art of it to any great degree. I wonder if there are exercises you can do to make yourself a better kisser? If there are, I bet they are pretty embarrassing.

Being pregnant is weird.

At what point do you stop being one person

and start being two?

It's weird, reading my origin story from the source documents. On blue-lined pages. How I came to be, laid out in ballpoint pen and smudges. Some of them were tears. We learned about all the different types of evidence that you need to do historical research in first year and I had to revise it for the exams this summer. It didn't actually come up or anything, so I suppose I didn't ACTUALLY have to revise it at all, but I did anyway. I think Mum's diary is a primary source, because she was there at the time, in the throes of it. But if you were going to write an essay or something about Mum (and why wouldn't you? – she was amazing) then my diary, if you could get your hands on it, would be a secondary source. Because I only really started keeping it regularly after she died. If you were writing an essay about me, my diary AND Mum's diary would both be primary sources. But I'm a bit crap, so I think that maybe your essay would have a limited audience.

Quote from Prim's mum's diary

Dad tried it on with other girls, probably even when he was engaged to her. He wasn't exactly smitten. Even she knew that and she was smitten with him. A suspicious kind of smitten, where she kind of knew it wouldn't work out well but hoped it would. I wish it had, while reading it. I wish that she had fallen for a less crap person than my stupid, gormless dad. He basically had no gorm at all when it came to her. He's not very good at romantic relationships. Maybe I get that from him. Although I could have tons of gorm. Never having had a proper boyfriend, it is hard to gauge how much gorm I do or do not have from a relationshippy point of view.

It must have been hard for Dad to read back over Mum's diaries. To see it all laid bare in blue and white what a horrid disappointment he had been. If he had given the diaries to me the year that Mum was killed I really think it would have broken me. Because I hated him for ages out of loyalty to Mum and also out of contempt for his parenting ineptitude. And I could muster up some hatred for him even now, only I'd still be stuck with him. My dad is all I have that will not leave me. Unless he dies or something, which could happen because he is an old dude. Fintan is fifty-three years old. Which isn't, like, super-old. But it is old enough that he has to take those tablets for his cholesterol and things.

The biggest thing my mum's death taught me is that parents aren't for ever. Their impact is, but that is not the same. Anyway, it wasn't fair the way he treated Mum, but how he's treated me since she died has been kind of nice with intermittent screw-ups. Or not so intermittent. Maybe it is because he has lived on his own for so long with no kids or womenfolk to guide him, but Dad is basically a teenager himself in a lot of ways. Only with wrinkles instead of acne and without even a modicum of cool. I'd like to see him meet somebody nice. Because when I go to college he'll probably regress to his before-I-lived-with-him levels of crapness. Only problem is, who'd have him? He's not the nicest boyfriend and is not getting any younger.

He does have **LOADS** of money, but the kind of lady who would be attracted by that wouldn't exactly be good to Dad, I reckon. He'd go back to buying ties that cost €250 and denying his farming origins. He never used to see his brother Patsy before I came to live there. Now we see them about twice a year. Which isn't loads, but it's definitely better than nothing. I'm always nice to them, because Mum's family are all dead and I have it at the back of my mind that if anything happened to Dad they'd be stepping up to mind me. I wouldn't like to have to move to Mayo. Two more years and then I can stop worrying about that, because if Dad died then, I'd be all by myself and have no-one minding me. I don't feel like I'll stop needing minding in two years' time. Maybe I will always need some level of minding.

OK, so there is this thing where the baby lives and it is called the amniotic sac. Which you think is revolting, until you hear tell of the mucous plug that stops the waters breaking and is basically a plug. Made of mucous. The human body is a mysterious and disgusting thing. Sorrel and me had to put the baby book under the sofa because we were both so creeped out. I don't know what I'll be like when I actually have a baby. But on the plus side, when the baby comes I will no longer be filled with amniotic sac and mucous plug. And placenta. Oh God, placenta! A placenta is basically an extra liver you grow around your womb to nourish the baby. Well, not exactly a liver, because then it would be called an extra liver. But big and meaty and able to break down things like a liver. Sorrel says she read about people in America who eat it once it comes out because it is filled with nutrients. We can't decide if this is more or less gross than the plug made of mucous. Probably more, but there's something about the word 'mucous' that makes it worse. I think when the baby comes, I will probably love it right away because I will no longer be pregnant and full of disgusting miracles. People look at me in the supermarket. At my big fat pregnant belly. I'm really glad of my engagement ring, which I wear whenever I leave the house to stave off eyebrows and moues of disapproval. I have an essay due on different translations of Sir Gawain and The Green Knight. I do not have time for this.

Quote from Prim's mum's diary

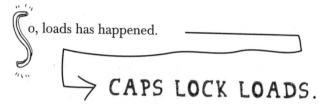

So, loads has happened.

CAPS LOCK LOADS.

I met Duncan for one thing. And the cinema visit with Robb was ∘ ∘ ∘ interesting. The kind of interesting that warrants three little dots in front of it. An ellipsis-y kind of interesting. But I'm going to start, not at the beginning because that would be predictable, but with what is, arguably, the biggest piece of gossip.

Ciara and Syzmon are no more. SHE BROKE UP WITH HIM. My hand actually had trouble writing that down because it feels so much like a lie. But it is the truth. She rang me, crying. I had never really thought of the dumper being sad when they dumped someone. I wonder if Dad was sad when he dumped Mum. I bet he was, a little. A sadness spiced with selfish. Like: 'I regret having to do this, but it was the right decision for the both of us,' or 'I could have handled that better.'

Ciara is of the 'I regret having to do this, but it was the right decision for the both of us' school of dumping. Her mum dropped her over to my house pretty much right away after the phone call. Ciara is a surprisingly loud sobber, and her mum was having her fibromyalgia support group over for coffee. Ciara's mum has fibromyalgia. It is a thing where you sometimes get really bad muscle pain and have to take to the bed. Ciara does the hoovering and toilet-scrubbing for her whole house because her mum doesn't want her fibromyalgia exacerbated and Ciara's dad is the kind of man who wouldn't say 'That's women's work' but would definitely think it.

'**WHY?**' was my main question for Ciara.

Because she properly loves Syzmon and he properly loves her. And fulfils at least **180** of her **234** requirements for a boyfriend.

'It wasn't because of **194**, was it?' (Syzmon has recently begun growing a sort of beardlet. He calls it a goatee, but 'beardlet' is a far more accurate term.)

'No. I would never dump someone because of **194**. Beards are so easily shave-able. It was because of loads of things. I mean, I still think that we'll end up together eventually.' She was trying to sound positive but her eyes were sad. I held her hand and squeezed it.

'Yeah?'

'Yeah. But I didn't want him to be my only boyfriend. And I kept on wanting to sleep with him, but I don't want to lose my virginity yet, because Mum goes through my drawers, like, all the time, and she'd go ape if she knew that I was even considering sharing my body with him.'

'But you've already shared loads of your body with him.' I refrained from putting air quotes around the body-sharing. She had enough going on without me criticising her word choices.

Ciara smiled a bit. Her lips curved anyway. There was some latent positivity bubbling under all the sad. I hoped it would come out soon. I didn't like her little crying face. It made me want to hug and I'm not huggy.

'I know, but I don't, like, give Mum a blow by blow account of it. I think she thinks we spend most of our time holding hands and talking about TV programmes we like.'

'So you broke up with him because you fancied him too much?'

This kind of blew my mind, but I held back from saying 'BUT WHHHYYYY?' because I'm tactful like that. She got it, though. Ciara understands the importance of having a boy to fancy. It is high on her list of priorities. Or was, at least, before she had this break-up.

She snuggled into the sofa and held her cup of tea in both her hands, like she was an old lady in the winter. 'Kind of. Any time I thought about losing it with him, I'd kind of also think about when I moved to London and he stayed behind and I'd get all sad and kind of wanting to stay in Dublin or follow him to Bratislava if he decides to go to college there and, I mean, if you're scared of the future all the time, that's no way to live, and I kept turning it all over and over in my brain until I decided the best thing to do would be to pull off the bandage.'

'Syzmon being the bandage.'

I looked at her. *Syzmon is not a bandage, he's a person,* said my look. *A person that you loved and stuff. You know?*

She wiped at her eyes and spread the make-up round them so her sockets looked like whirlpools with eyes inside the middle. 'I think I broke his heart, Prim. He properly cried and everything. I had to go downstairs and get him a glass of water.'

'Where did you break up with him?' I don't know why this seemed important. But it did.

'In my bedroom. I was going to do it in a public place, but then I wanted us to be able to have a proper chat about it without anyone looking or anything.'

'That was nice of you.'

'Syzmon didn't think so.' She started to cry again, big Hollywood tears bouncing down her cheeks one after the other. Ciara is ridiculously pretty, even when she's in bits. I think I would hate her if she weren't my second bestie. 'He said ... oh God, Prim, he said, he said ...'

'What did he say?'

'*If that's the way you feel.*'

'Wow.'

'I know. I never. I never thought he'd be so upset. I mean, I'm not that great.' She put her heavy head inside her hands.

'Yes you are, you're lovely. Of COURSE he'd be upset.'

'What if he gets another girlfriend? Oh my God, Prim.'

I curled my legs up underneath me. 'He won't for a while. He'll need time to heal.'

'I need time to heal.'

'I know you do. I know you do. Would you like a sausage sandwich and some Joy Division?'

'I'm not Fintan. I would like a cheese pizza and some *High School Musical*, please.'

'That sounds doable. I'll text Dad and ask if you can stay over. He'll totally let you.'

'I'll text Mum and see ...'

Dad said it was OK, but Ciara's mum needed her to do some house things, so she stayed till eleven and then Dad dropped her home. We had fun, interspersed with weeping. It takes a lot for Ciara to cry. I don't think I had seen her do it since Grandma Lily died the year before last. Maybe she cries when she is by herself, though. I mean, if I weren't me, I'd think that I didn't cry a lot. But I actually do. At least once a week. Usually when thinking about Mum, sometimes when thinking about Joel not being friends with me or Kevin not wanting me to be his proper girl-friend or the amount of time I will spend getting rid of unwanted body hair over the course of my lifetime. Time that could be better spent on snacking or reading books.

I hate using that stupid hair-removal cream on my legs and pits. It smells **SO WEIRD**. Shaving was much simpler, but Dad won't let me do it any more because he sucks. When I go to college, I'll totally shave again. And, I mean, it is nice that Fintan is trying to do some parenting. Laying down rules. Having concern for my well-being. All that nonsense. Look how far we've come since he was secretly going to propose to Hedda without telling me.

I wonder how Hedda is doing with her new, presum-ably childless husband and her new life? Probably fine.

She struck me as the kind of woman who would always do pretty well for herself, no matter what. No crying into ham and pickle sandwiches while pregnant with the child of a much older man who is inevitably going to dump you for Hedda. No shifting forbidden Kevins and then fighting with your best friend and then not being fancied enough to warrant anything beyond house party hook-ups and the odd text.

Kevin is not a very nice boy. I probably dodged a bullet. I wonder when a bullet will actually hit me? I quite want to get my heart broken nice and early to get it out of the way.

Although, looking at Ciara, maybe I could cope without any heartbreak for a while yet. She also timed the break-up perfectly. She didn't want to break up with Syzmon, or have just broken up with him, in Leaving Cert year. Because it would impact on their exam results and she wants him to be all he can be. Ciara over thinks things. But then again, you can't just go through life being surprised by the consequences of your actions, like they were something you had no control over. Something you couldn't help.

The man who killed my mum was one of those. He didn't mean to do it. He just did, and the end result is the same. Maybe if he had planned ahead and ordered a taxi before he started drinking, Mum would be alive today. I can get so stuck in those maybes. Maybe if she hadn't been all worried about her carbon footprint and bike-ridey. Maybe if it had been a nicer day, the visibility would have been better and she would have seen that he was driving dangerously and gotten out of the way. Maybe if the car had been going slower, or had hit her differently.

And then there are the other maybes. Maybe if Mum had been alive, I wouldn't have felt the need to cut myself. Maybe if Mum were alive, I wouldn't miss Roderick so much. Does that sound cold? He was like a furry little memory of her, you see. As well as himself. I wonder am I a smooth little memory of Mum for Sorrel? The kind of memory that smells faintly of hair-removal cream?

Syzmon must be gutted, the poor dude. I was going to text him, but I'd hate for Ciara to think I was putting the moves on him. I would not like to put a move on Syzmon. He belongs to Ciara and is not my type. Past history has shown that if he belonged to Ciara and were my type, it probably wouldn't stop me. God. I hate that Kevin completely eroded my morals, like as if my morals were limestone and he was water. Or a weak acidic solution that would also dissolve limestone. It's not that I am Karen or whatever. I chose limestone because it is one of the easier-to-dissolve sedimentary rocks. Karen's morals aren't even mudstone. They're like those vitamin C tablets that fizz up in water. I wish I had granite morals like Joel, or diamond ones like Ciara.

God, geography was a very boring subject. I'm glad I'm not taking it next year. For all that it's boring, though, sometimes it's nice to know things, random useless things you wouldn't ordinarily know. I mean, I had the whole

Internet in front of me for fourteen years before I found out about different types of erosion.

I think people get eroded too, by disappointment. Like, every time you get hurt, a little flake dissolves from off your heart and you're still able to hope and feel and love and all that. It's just – smaller. More guarded. Less of a leap. I don't know that there's anything you can do to stop it, though.

Ciara made the right decision. But Syzmon will be less now, because he knows about getting hurt by someone who loves you. And Ciara will be less, because she knows about hurting someone you love to save yourself from bigger, future hurts. Everyone is crumbling, like that story at mass about the woman who looked back and turned to salt. One shower's all it'd take.

So, I wonder who I'll talk about next. Robb or Duncan? Duncan or Robb? Robb has two bees but Duncan has Joel and is therefore more important. So we'll start with him. Joel and me were having tea and Duncan popped in to join us for an hour. Then he paid for the tea and cake and him and Joel left together to do kissing and things presumably. They said they were going to watch a movie. But I think if they were really going to watch a movie, Joel wouldn't have made don't-invite-yourself-along eyebrows at me.

Joel's eyebrows have a wide vocabulary. Duncan isn't as much of a sex predator as I had envisioned. For one thing, he looks younger than his age. And for another, he's quite unassuming. He kind of listened to Joel talk more than talked himself. But not in a creepy way. Although, an older man watching a boy with a view to fancying him is always going to be slightly creepy, just because of the age difference and the sexual intent.

I
KISSED
Robb.

Just thought I'd get that in there. It wasn't that great of a kiss. Is it weird that I felt it was, like, expected of me? Like he was an earl who had saved me from a highway-man and I was a lowly wench who had but one way to reward him – her virtue? I am reading the BEST Regency romance novel at the moment. I think earls might be my thing, the way Mum liked Vikings. Especially if said earls are also Egyptologists. I do still like Vikings, though. And certain knights.

Anyway, Robb was an earl because he expected things from me and, lo, he got them. Am I so easily won? While he was kissing me I was already telling Joel and Ciara about it in my head, like, *Look I have a life as well. Interesting things also happen to me.* That is not a good reason to kiss someone. No more

ROBBING

for you, young lady. I could feel his teeth. His oddly needley little incisors. I thought he was going to cut my tongue on them. I think I need to kiss another boy to stop Robb seeming like a viable summer-boyfriend option. No-one except him wants to kiss me, though. Because I amn't pretty and I suck at making friends.

Besides, I want to *experience* things and stuff. And if I'd only done kissing with people I fancied, I'd only ever have kissed one guy. And he didn't like me properly, so I feel there is a need to kiss other people to show him he is not important. Not that I still fancy him or anything. I don't. He is not important. I have moved on. I don't think I have moved on to Robb, though. I mean, I don't particularly want to be his girlfriend. He's a bit up himself. He paid for everything (which was a sign that kissing would be expected of me), so I suppose it's not a complete loss. Is that a dreadful thing to think? I actually am not short of a buck. I mean, Dad is loaded and even though he's big on making me earn a crust to teach me life skills, this is only in theory, because in actual practice he is too lazy/busy to do the proper kind of parenting that you read about in books.

Luckily, I was poor for the first thirteen years of my life. Not, like, living-in-a-garret, making-a-bag-of-rice-last-the-month poor, but the kind where, if I wanted to go on a school trip we had to look for something we could cut out. Dad paid maintenance for me, but Mum used that for big things like health insurance and saved the rest for college. She didn't like taking money from Dad. Reading her diaries, I can kind of understand why. Things went downhill pretty quickly after they got engaged.

I am teaching myself to knit. The baby will appreciate the fine clothes I will soon be able to make for it. Maybe it will impress Fintan as well. He caught me crying into a pair of tights that didn't fit me the last day. I was eating a sandwich at the same time and the tights were covered with pickle juice and tears. He put them in the bin and stared at me. It was not the stare of a man who thinks his wife-to-be will be a very good mother. It was not the stare of a man who thinks his wife-to-be will be a very good wife, as a matter of fact. I can't lose him. Being engaged is literally the only thing I have going for me at the moment.

So, Ella asked me to come over. But then she wasn't there at all. It was the weirdest thing. Felix was there, though. I think she might be trying to set us up. I know this because she said it, just after I rang the doorbell.

Quote from Prim's mum's diary

> I am not home at all. I have gone to town with
> Mum. I am trying to set you up. I hope you wore
> something blue. Felix likes blue. You're
> welcome.

I was wearing a black dress and a big orange hoodie with kitten ears growing out of the top. I looked like a jack-o'-lantern in drag. He asked me if I wanted tea, and I really did but I felt like I was going to puke and walked all the way home. It took ages and I was all sweaty and afraid.

How did I not know that he liked blue? I only have three or four blue things in my wardrobe. Mum's tea-party dress is blue. Light blue with fat dark-blue poppies on it. It is a kind of a magic dress that looks lovely on everyone. I feel like a lady when I wear it. A lady who wears little white gloves and goes for tea and has love affairs with wounded soldiers between the wars. It is only for special occasions. Seducing Felix with my average lady looks and moderately entertaining personality would be a special occasion, though. And by special occasion, I mean MIRACLE.

I kind of don't want to encourage this sort of thing. Because I've fancied him for so long that actually hooking up with him would be like making out with God or something. My poor flawed human body would not be able to process what was going on and I'd probably implode into a puddle of lady-goo and tears. I say implode because it is more decorous, knowing full well it would be an explosion and some would get on his T-shirt and probably not come out in the wash and how he would hate me then.

> Look Ella. I appreciate what you are trying to do.
> But please don't do it any more.

> Do you not like him?

How do you answer a question like that? Ella is very direct and I like to dance around the point and occasionally brush against it with an ankle in a flirtatious manner. I need to get sexier ankles. I have a big purple scar on the inside of my left one and it kind of looks like a flat varicose vein. Now, I'm no expert on what makes boys all wibbly and full of sex-lemonade in the tummy region, but I am, if not full sure, at least ninety-nine per cent sure that flat varicose veins are not the sort of thing people have fetishes about. I could do an Internet search and remove all doubt, I suppose, but I'm scared of what I'd find. I left the text unanswered for an hour until she asked again and then I was all,

> Ella. He's your brother. I cannot discuss any of my
> emotions with you at this time.

Which I thought was very ambiguous of me.

> He makes your elbows blush, Prim. I'm not exactly
> reading between the lines.

Nice use of idiom.

Don't patronise me.

Well, don't patronise ME then. Just because you are lovely and skinny and able to get with anyone you want does not mean you get to sort out my love life as well.

You are not fat, Prim. You're medium sized and some guys like that. And I don't think Caleb counts as anyone I want.

Have you fancied anyone since him?

No.

Then, 100% success rating.

I suppose so. Feel quite smug now.

You should. But not matchmaker smug. Desirable woman smug.

That is a good smug.

I wouldn't know.

Shut up, Prim.

Whereupon I did. I hope Ella doesn't meddle any more. I've liked Felix for so long that I feel it's kind of a magic secret, as opposed to a real thing that could happen. The power balance would be off. Because he would have all of it and I would have none. I think the power balance has to be equal in a relationship, with maybe a wee bit more fancying on the side of the person who is not me. At least to begin with. Mum's diaries have taught me a very valuable life lesson about power imbalances in relationships and what they get you. Apart from awesome girl babies who grow up into slightly less awesome teenage girls, that is. NATCH.

Fintan and I aren't speaking. I think he is having an affair with his secretary. He keeps working late and being out and not answering his phone or checking his answering-machine messages. I confronted him about it and he said I was being unreasonable. I didn't back down, for once, and now we aren't talking but we're still engaged and it is so weird and wrong and flawed and it is making me seriously unhappy. How can you be marrying someone who isn't speaking to you? Maybe I should call him and apologise. I'm probably being paranoid. Do pregnancy hormones do that? Probably. They seem to affect everything.

ad wanted to have a talk with me. He actually did have a talk with me. It was nice. Weird. Really weird, actually. But nice that he felt the need to talk to me about it. To ask my permission or whatever. It was to do with Sorrel. He likes her. Like, like-likes her. In that special way that men who fancy ladies get with ladies that they fancy. Which is almost impossibly weird but makes a kind of sense, if you look at opposites attracting and all that. Like, polar opposites.

Also, he was horrible to Mum. I didn't actually give him permission to ask Sorrel out. I said I'd think about it. Because it is so weird and I don't know if Mum would have liked it. In fact, I know she would have hated it. Sorrel probably wouldn't have ever gotten to hang out with Dad for any period of time at all if Mum were alive, because I would only have been with him on certain weekends still. Oh, God. The creepiness of it all. It is all **SO CREEPY**. And wrong. But at the same time I want him to be ... happy? And maybe she would be good for him?

It was not the most awkward conversation we have ever had. Mainly because I once had to explain what a moon-cup was to him. He thought it was a diaphragm and was asking me all these subtle are-you-having-sex-and-if-so-why-is-your-contraception-so-damned-retro type of questions.

Like, 'You know what a condom is, don't you, Primmy? It's a sort of a contraceptive sheath.'

Whereupon my ears started to bleed and I said, 'It's a moon-cup dad, it's a moon-cup. It is for lady-time, not for sexy-time. There have been no sexy times. There will be no sexy times for the foreseeable future. I will inform you in writing if I have need of any further such chats. Please leave.'

Which he duly did, fair play to him. Fintan is more than capable of taking a hint. Particularly when it comes in the form of an emphatic plea.

'Since when have you liked Sorrel?' I asked, because it is always good to know these things.

'Since ... for a while anyway.'

'Did you fancy her when you were going out with Mum?'

'NO. No. God, no. Why would you even ask me that?'

'Because I wondered. And I'm reading her diaries, wherein she is convinced that you are cheating on her.'

'I hated that bit.'

'Probably because you don't come off too well.'

'No. I really don't. I could have handled that whole business with your mum a lot better. I did apologise to her later on. But ...'

'She wasn't too into it?'

'No. No, she wasn't. Anyway, let me know what you think about Sorrel. Because I would like to ask her to go to dinner or something. But not if it would be ... problematic for you.'

'OK. Dad?'

'Yes?'

'I appreciate your telling me about this. It's decent of you.'

'Well, I'm trying my best at this full-time parent *craic*. I think we're doing pretty well actually. Now that we're used to each other.'

He smiled at me and I smiled back and felt a surge of love.

'Go Team Leary-Hamilton!'

'I am not referring to us as that.'

But, like all good fathers, when I held my hand up for a high five, he did not leave me hanging. I am going to get T-shirts made for us. And then insist he wear them. I know that means I'd have to wear them too, but it would be kind of worth it.

Robb texted me to say he missed boarding school and that there was nothing to eat in his fridge. He signed off with an x. It was a weird combination of boring and flirty. I mean, if someone is hoping to kiss you, as the x would imply, then why would they fill their text with only moaning? I texted him back.

> Sloths are tree-dwelling mammals with very little muscle mass. x

> Y r u talking about sloths to me? X

> Thousands of years ago, sloths lived on the ground and were as large as elephants. X

> They were not. x

> Were so. They leave their trees to poo, like once a week. X

> U r so weird.

> Sloths enjoy sleeping for up to twenty hours a day.

> Stop texting me about sloths. What u up 2? x

Sloths are excellent swimmers. They only have
their claws as defence against predators. X

I hate sloths. x

You can't hate sloths. Their main source of nutri-
tion is leaves. X

I wish I were a sloth. There is nothing in the fridge.
X

I think from now on whenever he starts in on boarding-school tales, I am going to bombard him with useless
facts about animals that I have learned from Ella or the
Internet. It will amuse me and it isn't really bullying
because proper bullying isn't edifying. Like, people don't
learn something while they are getting bullied. Ah, the
seductive dance of boy-texting. I have missed it so. I like
Robb with two bees better when he is a boy who is
texting me than I do when he is a boy who is in the room
with me in real life. It is perplexing. I hope I don't talk
myself into hooking up with him again out of boredom.
It is probably my destiny. Much like the destiny of the
sloth is to hang from a tree. Sometimes, even after sloths
are dead they hang from trees. Their claws are that powerful. I wonder, even after I am dead, if I will roll my eyes
when people say stupid stuff. That seems to be my most
powerful reflex.

The baby keeps kicking. It's moving more and more. Getting ready to escape into the world and be a person. I'm scared of what that will mean for me. I wonder will it bring me and Fintan closer together? That's an awful lot to put on a baby. But I would like if that happened, I think. I think I would like that a lot. To be a perfect little shining family together. For us to be a solid thing. A certainty.

Ciara came over. She was in bits. Syzmon is still having his house party. And he wants her to come. 'He wants all of us to be there, Prim.'

'That's grand, though, isn't it? I mean, you guys are supposed to still be friends and all that?' I don't know Syzmon all that well, but I am very invested in maintaining what few friends I have. And also, parties!

'I know. But I don't know if I'm ready to see him. What if I accidentally hook up with him?' She spread her hands out wide, like this was an innocent thing that could befall just about anyone.

Quote from Prim's mum's diary

'It's hard to accidentally hook up with someone,' I explained. I am a bit of an expert on this subject, as you will notice in a second.

'You accidentally hooked up with Kevin about seven times.' She made a pointy finger of accusation.

I raised an eyebrow. She had a point.

'Not all of those were accidents. They were kind of informed accidents. Or were they? I mean, I didn't want to with the clever bits of me, but then there were the needy-for-affection bits of me. And they won.'

'OK.' She didn't say OK like she meant OK. She said it as though it sounded dreadful.

'So my advice would be to amputate your needy bits pre-party.'

'That sounds painful.'

'Maybe you could make out with someone else instead? A sort of convenient substitute?'

'That would be really unfair on him, Prim. Oh, God. What if he does that to me?'

'Then we can leave.'

'OK. OK. We can do this.'

'We totally can.'

'Prim?'

'Yes, Ciara?'

'Can we do drinking at the party?'

'Of course we can.'

'I think that I would like something sugary that makes me not care about things.'

'Is there a drink for that?'

'I'm not sure. Probably. I have it in my head that it would be either blue or pink.'

'I'll see what I can do. Do you have ID?' I really want ID – it makes boldness so much easier.

'Yes! I have my cousin's college ID. She left it here when she visited and I nicked it from her wallet.'

'Ciara!' I was shocked and not a little jealous.

'What? They're less than a tenner to replace, and we gave her fifty for her birthday, so she's actually made a profit from our family.' She smoothed her skirt over her knees like that was the end of the matter.

'It's the principle of the thing. It is wrong to steal people's stuff.'

'Well, it was wrong of her stupid parents to go mental at me when Grandma Lily's will was read out.'

'Fair point.'

Ciara is funny. She's really moral in some ways and then she surprises you. It's good she has ID anyway. Wouldn't be getting any pink and blue drinks without it. Fintan only has whiskeys and wines and things. And they are not the most fun to drink. I hate the taste of whiskey. It feels like dirty sugar only burny. And whatever you mix it with, it overpowers. Maybe it will be an acquired taste, like blue cheese, which I also hate. I'm not prepared to work hard enough at it to acquire it any time soon, though.

Poor Ciara, I wonder if she will hook up with Syzmon at the party. It feels like she might. Particularly if there is drink involved. I'm not too gone on drink myself. Partly because my mum is dead because of it. And partly because I feel like this big responsibility to look after myself, because it's not like anyone else is going to. I mean, there's no-one who will properly mind me, tuck me into bed and take the day off work. Well, Dad will take the day off. But he tends to forget about me after a while and go to the bank or whatever else he needs to do. Is it weird that I want someone to dance attendance on me when I'm not feeling well? It is highly immature, for one thing. I should be stoic. I should be, like, ninety per cent more stoic than I am. As stoic as an aging cowboy. As stoic as a Victorian nanny. As stoic as a tree.

When I was thirteen, I thought that I would be so much wiser at sixteen. I remember really looking up to Felix, because he was in Junior Cert and practically a man. I don't feel any wiser, though. I feel the exact same, only with more boobs and general knowledge. Sometimes, I even feel a bit sillier. I mean, when I was thirteen, I had never cut myself or kissed the boy my best friend fancied first. I wonder when I will start to feel like I have a handle on this whole life business? Soon, I hope. I'd like it to be soon.

Joel is coming to Syzmon's party as well. He would like to bring Duncan. And Syzmon has said that it would be OK to bring him along. But Joel is worried that people will be there and that it will get back to Anne and Liam and that they will go ape and not let him have another boyfriend again till he is in college. This is a valid concern, because I kind of felt that way myself when I first heard about Duncan. Before I met him. And even now that I have, there's still this niggly little question mark that dangles over his head.

THE WHY ARE YOU DATING A SIXTEEN-YEAR-OLD WHEN YOU ARE A PROPER GROWN UP MAN QUESTION MARK.

I think I might need to invent a new sort of question mark for that. It will probably be wearing a trench-coat.

I don't know why trench-coats get such a bad rep, in terms of perversion. It is a versatile piece of outerwear. And by no means the only item of clothing that can be used to disguise nudity. I mean, that's basically the point of all clothes, ever. To one extent or another. I think I am going to wear my long-sleeved 1950s-style dress with the pouffy skirt and the sweetheart neckline to the party. It is lady-like but also makes me look thin and marginally classier than normal. Or maybe I should just go for jeans. I like standing out and being the only one dressed like me, but not to a creepy extent, where I'm dressed for a wedding when everyone else is dressed for a gig.

I wonder will Kevin and Siobhán be there? Syzmon gets on quite well with Kevin. He was going to start LARPing with us a while back. I don't know if he ever did. I haven't gone to anything with that crowd in months.

Fintan called. He said that he is sorry he was so harsh. And that he should have taken my pregnancy hormones into account. But that I should try to keep them in check and remember that there are two of us in it. That he is there as well. And that he didn't ask for this. It started out well, his apology. But by the end, I felt like I was the one who should be saying sorry.

Dolphin Laura called. She is going to Syzmon's party and wanted to know if I was going too, because it has been ages. It has been ages for a reason. I really like Dolphin Laura, but her boyfriend is the son of the dude who killed my mum, so I kind of get a bit itchy around her. A bit thinky.

Isn't thinking weird? Sometimes it's pure lovely, you get to wonder things like what life would be like if you were in a band on a world tour and what sort of music you would make and how you would answer questions in interviews. Or you can think about places to visit when

Quote from Prim's mum's diary

you are older. And you can think about your friends and how awesome they are and how lucky you are to have them, but all of a sudden it can swoop and it's like, If you were in a band, Prim, you would develop a drug problem and not a classy one where no-one has any idea for ages, but a messy one where you're wetting yourself onstage and saying outrageous things just to make people notice you and then you offend the wrong person and all of a sudden you're out of the band and they have a new lead singer/guitarist who is infinitely cooler and more popular than you (maybe Dolphin Laura or, in my worst moments, Karen) and none of them talk to you though you always swore you'd be friends for ever. Also, rehab is, like, super expensive, almost as expensive as maintaining a drug habit, so you're in a lot of debt and have to get a job as a janitor at your old secondary school and everyone looks at you and says things like 'How are the mighty fallen!' and 'You look ridiculous.' And places I'd like to visit can so easily swoop into places I will never get to visit with Mum. Or how will I support myself when I'm older now that Fintan has accustomed me to the finer things in life, like personal space and cheeses and little pots of pâté bought from cheesemongers?

And the friends thing is probably the most dangerous of all because you're, like, I'm so lucky to have such awesome friends, I'm so glad they like me for who I am and then you remember that who you are is dreadful and start analysing ridiculous things you have said and ultimately deciding that they are either friends with you as a cruel bet, which is unlikely because they are good people, and it would have to have been a long-running bet. Or they are too kind not to be friendly towards you. Because who else would have you and it sucks to be lonely. And they are kind, you know that they are kind. So out of pity.

Whenever someone is in a bad mood, I always find myself wondering if it is because of me, if it is something I have done, if there is a way for me to make it up to them. But sometimes people are just tired or bereaved or grumpy or whatever. I mean, it's really egotistical isn't it, to think that everything that happens to the people you love is, to some degree, because of you? But thinks are linked, woven together like crochet, singled and doubled and tripled in and out on top of each other and you don't know what your actions will mean, the things they can result in. All your actions loop around a hoop and then it pulls through other people's actions. There was a poem we did on a past paper about how no-one is an island, we are all interlinked, and I believe it but it doesn't comfort me. Because if we were islands, we could run our own island and do our best and sometimes maybe there would be ferries or even bridges, but we'd be far enough apart not to hurt each other so much every day. You know? Everything hurts. And certain thoughts are dangerous and so are certain tastes and smells and sounds that take you back to happier times that now are sad in retrospect. Or times that were just sad all by themselves. I never tell Dad what I get on tests. Because I got an A the day Mum died and I came home all proud. I don't want that to happen ever again.

I wonder do other people think like this? Dad and Ciara and Joel and Syzmon and Sorrel and everyone else in the world. Do they think like me? No wonder they're sometimes tired if they do. Being a human being is exhausting. And that's just the internal stuff. And there's so much outside stuff to do as well. Just being in the world takes up so much and most of it is 'cause of other people. Other people looping into the granny square of you, too strongly to unravel. I don't know whether to try to limit that or not. Sometimes all those loops inside your square are lovely and it feels like the cosiest rightest blanket in the world, and other times it feels loaded, like those influenza blankets the pilgrims in America used to swap with the Native Americans back in the day. Cosy, but ultimately fatal.

If I can survive losing Mum, I can pretty much survive losing anyone, I think. Thing is, I'm not sure I entirely survived it. I mean, I coped, but I amn't the same person that I was before it happened. I had been sheltered and loved all my life and I knew that the world was a bad place. I mean, I had seen the news and knew about war and death and cancer and all the other things that lurk in corners waiting for their moment but I didn't have first-hand knowledge. I wasn't a primary source.

On the plus side, sometimes there are parties.

Fintan forgot my birthday. He better not forget the baby's birthday, once it arrives. It's pretty exciting being 19. I am officially the oldest sort of teenage mother you can be. Sorrel says Fintan isn't worth it. What she doesn't understand is that he has to be. Because if he's not worth it then what do I have left? A baby I'm not qualified to care for.

And nothing.

Kevin is coming, so I texted Syzmon and asked if it was cool if I brought my new friend, Robb with two bees, to the party. He said that it was and asked if he should let Kevin know that I was bringing a boyfriend. Robb with two bees is not my official boyfriend, nor do I want him to be, so I said it wasn't necessary. If he were my boyfriend, I would have it tattooed on Kevin's face in mirror writing. *I found someone as well. Look. I'm good enough for someone else. A proper boy with arms and legs and everything.*

Quote from Prim's mum's diary

I also said that I was sorry to hear about him and Ciara. He said that maybe she would change her mind. Which, in fairness, maybe she will. I wouldn't hold my breath for it at this house party, though. I'm thinking that debs time might be a key re-kindler for them. Because princess dresses and true love seem to dance around together a lot in Ciara's brain, even if she is determined to focus on her millinery studies and not be in love with anyone for a while. I wonder who I'll bring to my debs. I'll probably go stag. Or can you only do that if you're a guy? Going doe isn't a thing at all. I think it's probably called going alone. Which sounds so much more desperate than going stag. I mean, stags get magnificent antlers. Alone people just get lonely. Well, I don't really get lonely by myself because of my incredibly busy head, but when I am by myself in crowds of people, or at a social gathering where there are loads of people who know each other better than I know them, then the lonely hits and I feel like a sore thumb. The dodgy uncle of the wedding party.

I wonder if it'd be OK to wear a costume to your debs? A girl this year wore a tux instead of a dress, and it looked quite cool. She wore red lipstick with it. But everyone was murmuring about her sexuality. As if trousers indicated anything at all about the shape of person you're attracted to. They're for covering legs, after all. I think I would like to wear a crown. Like, a big fat medieval crown, like the kind a girl would wear in her father's feasting hall before a Viking (with honourable intentions and a rippling set of abs) kidnapped her. As princess dresses and true love are to Ciara, so are crowns and Sexy Viking Kidnappers to Prim. I wonder if there was ever an earl who was also a Viking? I bet there was in a book. Books are so much more full of possibility than real life is. It is wondrous and frustrating at the same time.

Love?

Sorrel was up half the night puking her guts up. She was at a thing where someone had brewed his own mead with terrifying results. I asked her why she would drink that and she said that it smelt of danger-honey. At least, that's what I think she said. There was a whole lot of retching. I was up being pregnant and overly warm, so I got to mind her. At one point, she turned to me and said, "Bláth, you're going to be such a good mother. You have no idea how lucky ..." I think she was trying to be comforting or reassuring or something, but all she did was scare the hell out of me. I am not going to be a good mother. I am having trouble coming to terms with the idea of being any sort of a mother at all.

Quote from Prim's mum's diary

ONCE UPON A TIME THERE WAS A GIRL

is how a lot of fairy tales start. *Once upon a time there was a girl.* You don't have to suspend much disbelief to be on board with that. Always there is time and always there are girls. But one in particular who stands out makes you wonder why and that's why you keep listening. Boys in fairy tales normally come in threes. The first one, who gets it wrong. The middle one, who also gets it wrong, and then the last, who nails it and gets to marry the princess or inherit the kingdom or whatever. No-one ever expects the youngest son to amount to much in fairy-tales. But he always does. The older ones are stupid.

Girls in fairy tales don't come in threes. Except for Cinderella – the two ugly, the one beautiful. The two bad, the one good. But were they bad? Is it bad to listen to your mother, learn from her and do what you are told? And why not just call them mean? Why do people harp on at the ugly like it is a stick to measure women by? I always shine a little brighter when someone tells me I am pretty. That's because I know it isn't true. I have fooled them by being clever or being funny or being kind to them or something. That is how I get you and your eye adjusts and likes my face much more once it is the face of someone who has pleased you. People always think their friends are gorgeous. They think that because they are. Friendship is a gorgeous, gorgeous thing. And having it is lovely. And it is something you should really treasure. Because there are other people who aren't your friends. Those people owe you nothing and they see you with the eyes of cold observers.

In fairy tales there rarely is a girl with friends at first. Maybe she encounters helpful people on her path, her hero's journey. But almost always, always and at first she'll be alone. And there will be a bad thing coming. Bad things take many forms. There are monsters; there are wicked witches. Mothers die and kids are left alone.

I wonder if there's something dangerous in keeping a diary, making a story of your own life. Rewriting it a bit. Memories are never completely accurate, are they? And what's immediate can't be transcribed. Stories rarely middle happily, do they? They can begin that way and end that way, but there's always conflict necessary for the narrative to progress. And the middling. Well, that's the biggest part. One thing after another and another and another till the end. A series of climaxes and disappointments. When you write about yourself, do you make things worse or better? And if I think like this, why do I still do that? Am I so important, so worth writing about? Or is it just a filing cabinet, an external hard-drive for my brain?

Once upon a time there was a girl. And her mother died and she moved into a big house with her absent father. Seasons came and seasons went, and still the girl was sad about her mother. But as well as being sad she was growing up, shifting and changing into more of a woman shape than a girl shape. The things she worried about altered as well, some became bigger and others became smaller. Some of them were too big for her to fix all by herself and so her father paid a fairy doctor to sort her out and make her into the kind of girl who doesn't go in stories. The kind of girl who's happy all the time and everyone is friends with.

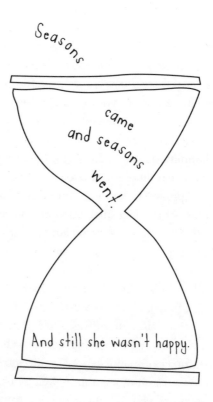

Seasons came and seasons went.

And still she wasn't happy.

Maybe the baby will give meaning to my life, I find myself thinking sometimes. Is that a very dangerous thing to think? Meaning seems like something so much bigger than a baby. Babies are very small, traditionally. But holding my watermelon tummy and imagining it dolphining around in the amniotic fluid, my baby feels like it will be big, enormous, impossibly huge, the biggest thing in the world.

I read somewhere once that alcohol kills brain cells. When my head was sore this morning, I stared at the unfamiliar ceiling and tried to remember interesting facts about the Industrial Revolution (1760–1840). There are no interesting facts about the Industrial Revolution because the gist of it is basically: there were more machines that did stuff and that made stuff easier to do. Also, this dude called James Hargreaves invented the Spinning Jenny and everyone thought he was impossibly cool. Other people invented other stuff also, and they were all very pleased with themselves in Britain. In Ireland, we were still all rural and living the sad lives of share-croppers and so on and so forth. Ulster had an Industrial Revolution. The rest of Ireland had an over-reliance on potatoes until the famine. As I was pondering this, Ciara came into the room with a pint glass of water.

'Here you go,' she said, looking at me as though I were a little fawn who might escape if not spoken to gently enough. I *felt* kind of like a little fawn who might escape if not spoken to gently enough. All woozy and delicate and things. We hadn't planned on staying over in Syzmon's, had we? Why were we still here?

'What year is this?' I demanded, getting the most important question out of the way first thing.

'You have not time-travelled, Prim.'

'Then why am I not where I am supposed to be?'

'You got drunk.' She pursed her lips.

'Oh,' I said. She nodded.

'Yes.'

'Did you also get drunk?'

'Not *as* drunk. I'm not sure anyone could have got as drunk as you got last night and not died. It was pretty impressive.'

Oh God.

'Did I make a fool of myself?' I asked, already knowing the answer.

/   /

O O O

'No. NO. It was kind of when almost everyone had left. And I put you to bed. And I told Mum I was staying over at yours and your dad that you were staying over at mine.'

'Thanks, Ciara. You are the best.'

'You're welcome.' She looked at her hands. They were in her lap. Her nails were robin's-egg blue and filed into little ovals.

Another question rose inside my gut. 'What did I do?'

She narrowed her eyes. 'Tell me what you remember doing and I'll fill you in.'

I did not like the sound of this at all. 'Ciara?'

'Yessy?'

'Can I have five more minutes in bed?'

'No. You're having a shower and then we're having a big chat and then we're meeting Mum in town at four o'clock.'

'Oh.'

And that's
when I realised
I wasn't wearing

any pants.

When do memories begin exactly? I have one or two from when I was a toddler but not many. So there's a small window of opportunity to get things wrong before the baby remembers enough to hold a grudge.

Quote from Prim's mum's diary

My head felt full of ink instead of thoughts. I have never not remembered anything before and it was really scary. I had a bit of a memory. I mean, I know how the night began.

Fintan and I visited Mum's grave that morning. We brought her flowers. It had been two weeks. We normally go once a fortnight now. It used to be every week, and then it changed. I wonder if by the time I'm eighteen we'll even make it once a month? It will be harder to do when I'm in college.

What happened was basically that there was a party. Nora came without Karen, who had not been invited but still shows up later. If a party is good enough, Karen just manifests at it. You don't even need a Ouija board to summon her or anything.

Ciara and I had obtained pink and blue drinks. They were very sugary. The blue drink was a sort of vodka thing that was fizzy and tasted of cheap ice-pops and the pink drink was a sort of wine and seven-up hybrid, only pink. We mixed them together to see if they'd go purple, but they didn't and when we thought about it later, we realised that it had been a foolhardy endeavour. At the time, though, it felt very scientific and important. James Hargreaves knows what I'm talking about.

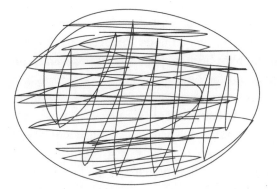

And the next morning I woke up with no pants on. Which I am getting to. But what good is a horrible experience if you can't dance around the telling of it? I am still putting together theories. I mean, I amn't sure what happened. I mean, I have an idea. I have a definite idea. But I amn't fully sure. My idea isn't something that I'm gone on. I mean, I don't think I just took off my pants all by myself, because of the heat or whatever.

How can you tell if you've been *interfered with*, as Ciara put it in her Grandma Liliest of tones. Is it something you're supposed to sense, to just know? Because everything is ink, it's covered up in ink and I can't see it. Jesus. I am so frustrated at myself for getting drunk. I knew no good would come of it. I knew. And yet. Oh, decision-making skills, I would definitely not have got an A in you in the Junior Cert.

I wish you could get grinds in not being a screw-up. I suppose that's what the CBT is supposed to be, but I am NEVER telling Caroline about this ever. I am SO embarrassed. Anyway. So. There were drinks. And Ciara and I were drinking them. Apparently, Ciara had every bit as much as me. I had assumed that I would have a higher tolerance for alcohol than her because she is a tiny pixie and I am a massive goblin. But no. Pixies can put it away, apparently. Goblins begin to puke after their seventh cup of either pink or blue drink.

Initially, goblins are great fun and everyone loves them. They go dancing with older-man perverts and are very good about judiciously ignoring Siobhán and Kevin, who apparently could not take his eyes off a certain goblin all night. I am calling myself a goblin here because it helps to distance me from my actions. I did not do it. A goblin did it. A goblin called Steve. OK, so henceforth in this story, I will be played by a goblin called Steve.

<u>Cast</u>

Primrose Leary...Steve, the Goblin

Because actual people would have been a lot cleverer in terms of their decision-making skills than Steve the goblin was in this story. Steve has made some dreadful life choices in his/her time, but never has he felt more thoroughly humiliated than he did last night. Steve the goblin was initially quite normal and happy and doing a good job of keeping Ciara away from Syzmon. Steve went to the bathroom to inexpertly reapply her eyeliner and when she came back, Ciara and Syzmon were in the garden, having the kind of deep and meaningful conversation that goblins are not welcome at. Steve the goblin thought a bit about whether they would hook up and, if so, would that mean that they got back together and she concluded that it would. Because Ciara is not exactly the kind of girl to break someone's heart twice in one week. At least Steve thought so. Poor foolish Steve, the drunken goblin.

'Oh, Steve,' you are probably thinking, 'surely it can't have been that bad.'

To which Steve can only sit with his head in his hands, murmuring incoherently, his sorrow and shame floating out like seaweed on the ocean of what a useless person he is. WHAT A NAUGHTY GOBLIN I HAVE BEEN! thinks Steve.

What an utter disappointment I've become!
I'm glad my mother's not around to see me.
I am glad I am not a human being,
because the social fallout from this
would be devastating.

Steve the goblin met his best friend Joel the person at the party. Joel was there with his boyfriend and Steve and Joel went out into the garden to have a smoke. Neither of them smokes, but they wanted to have a bit of a gossip. Sometimes, the best part about being romantically involved with someone is dissecting them fondly like treasured pigs that have lived a life and now must turn to chops.

So Steve shared a cigarette from a packet Joel had bought on a night out with Duncan's friends, so he would have something to do with his hands when he felt awkward, and they talked. Joel thinks that he's in love. And Steve is happy for him, he really, properly is. But he is also a goblin conflicted, because the age gap is big. It's not big when we're twenty or we're thirty, but it's too big now and I've read about my mum and how things went down there, and I'd hate him to feel used.

'I think that, if it breaks up, I will feel used,' he said, 'but I would even if Duncan was our age. I think that every relationship you have will disappoint and empty you, until one doesn't, and, while I don't think we're going to be civil partners and adopt a kid and everything, he makes me happy for now and I really fancy him. And it's not like I'm going to get pregnant. So what's the harm?'

Steve shook his goblin head. 'I don't know what the harm is, exactly. But I strongly feel that there is a harm there. Lurking.'

'Ugh. I hate lurking. Kevin was really good at lurking.'

'He was, wasn't he? He'd lurk and he'd lurk, and then somehow I'd find myself kissing him.'

'Not any more.'

'Nope.'

Joel the person tilted his head in a regretful manner. 'He used to be a nice guy, you know. Remember the LARPing?'

'Who could have predicted he would not be the perfect boyfriend?'

'No-one. I mean, he was sometimes a Jesuit assassin.'

'A HOT one at that,' mused Steve the goblin. 'Let us speak no more of Kevin, Joely. It cuts deep.'

'Like the blade of a vampire ninja.'

'I never want to fight over a boy again.'

'And I never want to fall for a straight boy again. I don't think we can exactly plan these things, though. But I would hope that next time, you might not kiss him all over his face without discussing it with me first.'

'I hope so too. I get very distracted by kisses. I'm worried I'll grow up to make poor life-choices or become a sex-pervert.'

And, though Steve the goblin did not know it, his words were oddly accurate. For some very poor life-choices were to be made by him that very night.

Joel, too, was making life-choices that were arguably rash. For he left early to repair to Duncan's flat (Duncan has his own flat, that he lives by himself in, because he is old, old as Methuselah) for the purposes of kissing and other nice things. Steve the goblin missed Joel. And Ciara, who was still engaged in chat with Syzmon. They kept doing hugging. Not sexy hugging, but supportive, friendshippy hugging. Steve longed to know what they were banging on about out on the patio. For he was a curious goblin, prone to poking his nose into the business of pixies and other woodland creatures. This was mostly because Steve had very little going on in his life and also had a lot of time on his hands.

Before the boy and his friend the grown-up man headed off, Steve had another drink and did some crazy dancing with Duncan while Joel used the bathroom. (I am flittering around the night piece by piece because it is like trying to cobble together a mind-jigsaw using only your elbows.) Steve observed that Duncan was quite the adept dancer, capable of doing lots of dipping and twirling manoeuvres that made a gal feel all graceful. Steve reminded herself that she was not to fancy the same people as Joel any more and glared at Duncan until he asked her if there was something in her eye. She told him there was an eyelash in her eye because there could have been. How was he to know with his old-man ways and his young-man boyfriend?

Steve had another drink. Ciara returned.

'I'm taking a break from chatting to Syzmon,' she exclaimed. 'Lest I accidentally kiss him. Let's do shots.'

This was most unlike Ciara. It was almost, Steve thought later in retrospect, as though she wanted to get absolutely trolleyed so she would have an excuse to hook up with Syzmon. At the time, however, Steve was not into it.

'I don't know.'

'Ah, come on. It will be fun.'

'Don't you peer-pressure me, Ciara.'

'I will. I will peer-pressure you into an early grave. Have some cocaine while we're at it. And a bit of heroin.' Ciara was emphatic.

Steve was clearly going to have to use every bit of his moral fibre to resist.

'Ooh, now that you mention it, I could totally go for some heroin.'

'I don't have any on me. You'll have to have a shot instead.' Ciara's eyes were wide and impetuous.

Steve was powerless against her. That's how they get you. Your peers. By being friendly spiced with crazy eyes.

'A shot of what?' Steve asked.

'Syzmon has a GREEN drink. It tastes like applejacks.'

'Green drink? But what about pink and blue?'

'I have decided green is also acceptable,' said Ciara wisely.

'Fine.'

'Fine?'

'Come on, before I change my mind.'

'You are the bestest, Prim. I love you.'

'Love you back, silly girl.'

Ciara says things like 'I love you' like it is not a hard thing to say or to feel. I didn't say it back to her the first time she said it to me. But now I do occasionally. Just so she knows that I think she is amazing. It's weird, saying it to more people. I say it to Joel and sometimes Ciara. Rarely Dad. He knows I love him, though.

Anyway, back to Steve. Our goblin friend had a little bit of the apple drink and it was quite nice, but she didn't want to get drunk and something her mother had said when she was little came back up through her brain like the things she drank would later do in her mouth and oesophagus. Oh, goblin Steve, you are a silly goblin. Sometimes you make the right choices swiftly followed by the wrong ones. And then find yourself pants-less and sorry.

Ciara wanted to dance. She seemed really happy, almost like she was working at it. She was vivacious in a way I hadn't really seen before. She was having a good time so people would see her having a good time and know that one was being had. I'm very good at spotting underlying misery. So is Steve. Steve wanted to help Ciara, to be a good friend. Steve also enjoyed fun, because what goblin doesn't?

Then Kevin the troll walked in, with his girlfriend Siobhán the elf. Siobhán had been on holidays with her family earlier in the summer and she was all tanned and golden, like a statue or a girl from an ad for expensive T-shirts. Steve hated Siobhán the elf. She hated her pointy ears and her gossamer wings and her stupid little laugh. Most of all she hated the way she acted around Kevin the troll. Like she owned him. Like he was the most fascinating slave in the world. 'You can't own a troll,

Siobhán,' Steve wanted to exclaim. 'And anyway, I had him first. He put his mouth on my mouth several times. *Several times*, elf.'

Steve refrained from exclaiming anything at anyone. For the moment. Later, there would be a marginal amount of exclaiming. I think. When faced with a troll who you used to do kissing with, a goblin must be very brave indeed. You don't need a sword or anything. But you do need to be quite friendly. So the troll won't suspect that you are hurting. It isn't that Steve still liked the troll, mind you. Nothing like that. It's just that Steve liked to be good at things. To win. And in the game of who-can-be-the-troll's-favourite, he had lost big. So Steve nodded and said 'Hi' and 'How are you?' and asked Siobhán about her stupid holiday, like his heart was made of sinew instead of muscle soft as mollusc, maybe softer.

Laura the queen of the fairies entered at this point. She did not have her queen's consort with her, and this made Steve the goblin feel relieved and also sad. The queen's consort was every inch as beautiful as she and quite as regal. But his father had slain the little goblin's mother with a big sword made of car, and Steve the goblin did not like being reminded that he still existed. Steve was of the opinion that people should be able to disappear, to puff out like smoke if you hated them hard enough. It would have made Steve's life a good deal easier were that the case.

Steve chatted to the queen of the fairies for a while, but everyone wants to chat to fairy queens and she was bundled off by other people, which made Steve happy. Because no matter how much Steve liked the queen of the fairies, the business with her boyfriend's father hung between them in the air like a bad smell. Worse than a bad smell. A stench. Like a painful stench was how it hung and it was hard for Steve to pretend that the stench wasn't there when it so clearly was. Steve had another drink. It is at this point, in retrospect, that Steve should have stopped drinking, the drunken man who killed his mother like a lesson for him. But goblins are not known for their wisdom, and so Steve drank and looked around the room, and spotted Felix. He was there with several of his friends and also Ella. Steve went over to Ella.

'Hello, Steve the goblin,' said Ella.

'Hi, Ella,' said Steve the goblin.

'I am not drinking but I still slightly want to kiss Caleb,' said Ella.

'That is not a good idea,' said Steve. 'You will hurt his feelings'

'I won't. I'll only kiss him. I won't say anything mean. Everybody else is kissing people and it's like when it's sunny and everyone has ice-creams and even though I'm not a fan of ice-cream I want one too.'

'Don't eat ice-cream, Ella.'

'The ice-cream is a *metaphor*, Steve,' said Ella. 'Also, I brought Felix for you. He thinks he's minding me and drinking things, but I am going to set the two of you up and it will be delightful.'

'No it won't. Robb with two bees is coming.'

And it was true. The two-beed knight was approaching on his horse even as Steve spoke. He brought a smile and a brown paper bag filled with little hotel bottles of drink. They were for sharing. Apparently his parents were always getting them in hampers and never kept proper track. Or something. Steve the goblin was suspicious. Steve was always a little suspicious when people offered her things. What will you want in return? the little goblin thought. Is it something I'm prepared to give you?

The goblin looked at Felix. Felix looked back and he did that thing with his eyebrows that means 'Hi' and 'Are you OK?' in equal measure. Steve nodded and approached the two-beed knight.

'Looking well, Steve the goblin,' said Robb the knight. He put his hand on the small of Steve's back and the goblin hoped that Felix hadn't seen and Kevin had. She kind of wished that Felix wasn't there so she could do pointed kissing with Robb on a variety of sofas.

'Hi, Robb,' said Ciara.

Ciara had not met Robb before. But she knew about the kissing.

'Hi, Robb,' said Ella, who had also heard about the kissing.

Steve introduced her friends to Robb and he gave them little bottles of drink as presents. Ciara was enchanted with hers. Ella put hers in her handbag. 'I do not drink, but I am going to put this bottle beside Mr Cat and take some photographs. For the laugh.' She said 'for the laugh' the way another person would have said 'for the purposes of important scientific research' and her brow furrowed a little with the planning.

Sometimes Steve's small goblin's heart glowed with love for Ella.

Suddenly, there was a clap of thunder and a flash of lightning and the whole room filled with brimstone and sulphur. A carriage driven by a headless horse-man pulled up and the devil herself emerged, clad in a little silken sheath and a push-up bra that made the devil's boobs look like a threat. Steve the goblin's stomach did a flip. She hated the devil. The devil was always causing trouble.

'I am going to go to the garden,' announced Steve, 'to get some fresh air.'

And so she did.

In the garden, Steve encountered the devil's ex-girl-friend Nora the person. Nora was upset. She glared at Steve, as though Steve were a more disgusting goblin than he actually was. The kind that gobbles children.

'I'm sorry,' said Steve. 'I don't know if I ever said a proper sorry to you. For what I did to Karen.'

Steve had not announced anything about Nora to the whole school over the intercom, but Nora's eyebrows seemed to be asking for something. Something Steve had got increasingly used to giving people over the past year. Steve the goblin was very good at apologising. The world was a place where he was increasingly at fault.

'You don't need to apologise to me,' said Nora the person, but if Steve had looked up that sentence in a the-saurus he would have found 'You totally do' and 'You are a terrible person' sitting beside it like friends.

'I just ...' said Steve. 'I just really hate the devil.'

'You mean Karen,' said Nora.

'Yeah,' said Steve, 'I do. She's so *mean*. And not mean like she can't help it. Mean like it's a hobby and I'm sure that she was perfectly nice to you but she was mean to me about my mum. My mum died when we were in primary school and Karen said some things and also some things about Ella and she's just mean and I don't like her, so that was my motivation for doing the thing that I did. Which was wrong and also mean as well and I am sorry.'

'Mam calls that "sinking to her level",' said Nora.

'Dad does too. It's not supposed to be a good idea, but what else can you do?'

'Ignore it.'

'They A L W A Y S say that, don't they?' said Steve.

Nora nodded. 'Ignore it and they'll get tired and go away.'

'Like they were toddlers.'

'Toddlers don't work like that,'

'Oh. I wouldn't really know. I haven't been a very successful babysitter. There was an incident.' Steve had besmirched the honour of a family baby and had not been let babysit by himself since.

Nora had an undercut and little eyes that were an orange kind of brown. Her nail polish was chipped and one of her ballet flats had a bit of sock poking through it.

'I babysit all the time. I have, like, twenty cousins.' Nora passed Steve a brown paper bag. It had a bottle in it.

'I always like to drink out of a brown paper bag,' said Nora. 'For effect.'

Steve took a drink from Nora's magic bottle. It tasted like potion. Not very nice, but you can tell that it is going to *do* something to you and that makes it palatable.

'Karen and me were together for three months,' said Nora. 'Like, not officially. But then kind of officially. And then we weren't. She didn't even break up with me. She just stopped being my girlfriend and I was all, "I don't know what I've done," and "Tell me what I did," and I texted and emailed and messaged and she blocked me on the things, on all the things. And I don't know what I did.'

'Maybe you did nothing.'

'But that's nearly worse,' said Nora, who was surprisingly wise for someone who had dallied with the devil in a sexual manner. 'Because, if I did nothing, it means she just got sick of me. And I do not want to be a thing you can have too much of and then get sick of. I don't want to have, like, an expiry date. And she's kissing boys again now. And probably girls as well, but those are harder to find than boys – the ones who'll kiss you, I mean. And she's beautiful and scary and powerful and I liked her so much. I think I properly loved her, even. And now she's out there, looking like she looks, and I am sitting on the ground, talking about her, which I know that she can *sense*, and she doesn't care and my shoes aren't working and please have another drink of this, Steve the goblin. Because if I drink it all I'm going to puke.'

Steve took another drink of the potion, which apparently was some sort of emetic.

'Have you considered pink and blue drinks at all?' he asked Nora.

Nora hadn't. And so the goblin and the person sat, and Nora talked some more about the devil. And the goblin spoke of Kevin and his ways and means and suggestive throaty laughter which bubbled from within and made Steve cross. Because it isn't nice to laugh when you are a bad person.

'Bad people should not be allowed to enjoy themselves,' said Steve the goblin.

'Karen's not a bad person, though.'

Steve looked at Nora.

'Not entirely. I mean, she really helped me deal with certain things. She listened. I came out to my parents because of her. Because of what happened at school. And they were great. I mean, they're really supportive and everything. I'm not allowed to tell my nan, though.'

'Why not?'

'They don't think that she has very long left, and they don't want her last years on earth to be spent reconciling her religious beliefs with her lesbian grand-daughter.'

'Oh. That seems like it should not be their decision to make.'

'Well, I'm their child so I get to do what they tell me.' Nora sighed. 'Wish me luck. I'm going in.'

Steve the goblin took off her shoes and gave them to Nora. Their feet were the same size, which was lucky because over-sized shoes would have been equally as ridiculous as holey ones.

'Thanks, Prim,' said Nora to Steve the goblin.

'You're welcome,' said Steve.

The sky was the kind of dim it is when day is making up its mind whether to go to bed or not. Steve felt like he had made, if not exactly a new friend, then definitely a new not-enemy. Which was almost as good, and maybe even better. It was nice to have fewer enemies, thought Steve, walking barefoot into the party like an old-timey tramp.

Steve walked back into the party. Ciara grabbed her arm. 'OK. I have had a mad idea. And it might be too mad, and it might make you mad at me, but it might actually be good for both of us.'

'Hmm?'

'So, you know how you are conflicted about whether or not you like Robb?'

'I'm fairly sure I don't like him. I just keep kissing him. I mean, he's grand. I don't mean I don't like him. I just don't ...'

'Want him?'

'Yes.'

'OK, so.' Ciara took a swig of pink drink from a little plastic cup like they have at children's birthday parties. 'I think I should kiss him.'

'So I don't kiss Syzmon. It would, like, break us up definitively. Once and for all.' She eyed Robb, who was going through the DVD shelf like he owned the place. He might have been alphabetising. He was definitely up to something.

'Why does everyone want to kiss everyone else?' Steve wondered.

'Because we are teenagers,' said Ciara, 'and only get let out on occasion. Things build up.'

'You only broke up with Syzmon a week and a half ago.'

'I know. But I've been with him for three years, almost. Oh my God. I've only ever kissed one boy. I could like **DOUBLE** my number.' She eyed Robb again. 'And he's quite cute.'

Steve the goblin shrugged his shoulders. 'If you go for that sort of thing.'

'The ridiculously hot thing?'

'No. The dissolute-younger-son-of-an earl-who's-prob-ably-going-to-knock-up-the-scullery-maid sort of thing.'

'You read too much. Am I allowed to kiss him?'

'Of course you are, but I am worried about your heart and Syzmon's. I am worried it will be a bad move.'

'It might be.' Ciara adjusted the waistband of her skirt so it sat exactly right. 'But if you don't move you stagnate and stagnation is death. We are like sharks, Prim. Like sharks.'

'Um?'

'I just want to make sure, though,' said Ciara. 'That I won't be hurting your feelings. Because your feelings are important to me because you are my best friend in the whole world. I know Joel is your best friend, but you are my one.'

'Oh, Ciara.'

'So, is it OK?'

I nodded. 'Yes, but are you sure?'

But she was already gone. Steve the goblin looked after her.

Ella grabbed Steve's arm. 'Come out to the garden! I have news!'

The garden was obviously the place where news got told. Steve and Ella passed two other huddles, deep in conversation. Things were happening. Dynamic, world-shattering things.

'So. I asked Caleb if he wanted to do kissing with me and he did. And we did kissing.'

'Oh. Where?'

'Prim! Mostly on the face and neck.'

'No, I mean – in the garden? Where is the kissing place?'

'We used Syzmon's parents' en-suite bathroom. It was pretty romantic. They have a skylight and little furry toilet-seat covers.'

'Ooh!'

'I know, right?'

'Ciara asked me if she was allowed to kiss Robb with two bees.'

'She's not allowed to kiss Caleb. We're back together.'

'Really?'

'Yes. I asked him if he would be my boyfriend until the twenty-ninth of August.'

'So, it's like a short-term thing?'

'Yes. I have plenty of spare time at the moment and I can help him with his ferret and we can go on lovely dates and things. And then, once school starts I'll be busier and I won't want a boyfriend any more.'

'Right. And he was OK with that?'

'He was. He likes having me to talk to and hang out with, and we're friends anyway, so it's like we'll just hang out way more and also do kissing.'

'That sounds really nice.'

'I know. I'm pretty pleased I thought of it. Anyway, Mam is coming to pick me up in half an hour. So if you want to make a sexy move on Felix, now would be the time.'

'Ella!'

'What?'

'Does it not gross you out that you are basically trying to, like, pimp me to your brother?'

'No. It would only be gross if I were, like, going to watch or something.'

'That would be gross.'

'Very.'

Steve and Ella took a moment to process how disgusting that would be.

'Steve?'

'Yes, Ella?'

'I sometimes wish I could bring Mr Cat to parties. I wish that was, like, a normal thing to do.'

'I used to wish the same thing about Roderick. Particularly just after Mum.'

'Do you miss him?'

'Yes. A lot.'

'And her as well?'

'Yeah. I got her diaries on my birthday and I've been reading them, but a diary isn't the same as a mother. It's smaller and full of writing instead of life.'

'I wish your mum hadn't died.'

'Me too.'

'I wonder if we'd still be friends if you hadn't moved in with your dad?'

'I think we would. I'm fairly sure. Maybe not as close, though.'

'I like being friends with you.'

'Me too.'

Syzmon came into the garden. He looked worried.

'Where is Ciara?'

I was worried that Ella would tell him, but she looked down at the ground the same as me.

'I think she was over near the DVDs?'

'With your boyfriend?' he said hopefully.

'Robb's not my boyfriend.'

'Oh,' Syzmon said and if you looked up that 'oh' in the thesaurus a lot of words for really, really sad would have been nestled in beside it.

'Will you drink with me, my friends?' asked Syzmon.

And Ella said she didn't drink, so he went to get her a Coke instead of cider and Steve the goblin should also have switched to Coke at this point but she didn't because Syzmon brought out blue drink for her, Ciara having absconded to God-knows-where with the pink drink. We all sat down. One of the other huddles had left. The moon was coming out, the sky wasn't exactly a night sky yet, but it was definitely getting there. Days are really long, Steve the goblin thought. It feels like this day should be a night now. It feels like it should be over. But it wasn't. More things were to come. More things always came. Steve was going to be filled with things by the end of the night. Things that she would have to process slowly. More things that she wouldn't be able to process at all, because she couldn't remember them.

(Steve spent the best part of the day after the party sending texts to people along the lines of 'So ... what was

YOUR favourite memory of me from last night? Because I seem to have lost quite a few of mine.')

But back to the evening, or the young night maybe? Steve the goblin didn't have a watch. Almost ten, perhaps. She hadn't asked anyone for the time during the course of the night, because if the time was important, someone would probably have told her what it was. He, I mean. Steve is a boy's name. Maybe if you are a goblin, it could be a girl's name. Maybe goblin gender is more fluid. Don't be silly, goblins aren't real. Except for Steve, of course.

After a bit of talking about generic summer things, Ella had to go outside to her mum and Syzmon pounced. Steve had known that the pounce would happen. Because, were he in Syzmon's lily-white runners, he would have pounced.

'Did you know?' asked Syzmon, and if he had been an earl or a sexy Viking it would have been at the point in the novel where a window was behind him and a storm outside was reflecting his feelings and his shirt would have been rumpled and his eyes wild. His eyes were a bit wilder that normal, but Syzmon has very gentle eyes, so it wasn't, like, intimidating or anything. The sad thing is, though, that the ladies in romance novels would usually get back together with their Viking. But Steve didn't think that Ciara would get back with Syzmon. At least not until she was a famous milliner with plenty of stability and time.

'I did not know,' I said. 'She rang me after and I was really surprised. I didn't see it coming.'

'Me neither.' He took a long swig of his drink. 'It is hard. I see her and I want to touch her and look at her and I am not allowed to. It is very hard.'

'I know. I mean, I haven't had a relationship as long as you and Ciara, or anything at all important really. But I find it awkward being around Kevin. It is like, normally, you just are you. The normal level of yourself and it is fine. But when confronted by a certain type of person, you find yourself trying to act normal instead of actually being normal. And it is hard.'

'She misses me,' said Syzmon and his eyes were sad.

'I know she misses you.'

'Then why can't we get back together?'

Oh, Syzmon, thought Steve the goblin. *You do NOT want to go next nor near your parents' en-suite for the fore-seeable future.*

Steve patted Syzmon's back in an inadequately comforting manner. 'It'll be OK.'

'No. It won't. I mean, it won't. Did she tell you why she broke up with me?'

'Because she would have to eventually and this was easier?'

'Yes. Isn't that the stupidest thing you have ever heard? I mean, I did not tell her that I thought that she was stupid. Because she gets enough of that at home. But, really? I mean, really? I am her best friend. In the whole world, I am her best friend. And she breaks up with me because she is scared that some day she will have to. That is not good enough. Not good enough at all.'

'No,' said Steve, because it kind of wasn't.

'Could you talk to her for me? Ask her why?'

'The why she told you is why, Syzmon. There is no deeper reason. She didn't do it lightly. She was really upset.'

'I know she was. But she didn't have to be. I don't have to be feeling any of this. But it's up to her to fix it and I can't make her and it is very hard. I hoped tonight. I shaved my goatee off. I bought new runners.'

He had bought new runners. They shone through the dusk like sporty beacons. I didn't know what to say. So I offered Syzmon blue drink. He was not a fan.

'It tastes like those horrible iced-pops that come in the plastic tube. The blue kind.'

'Mr Freezes?' asked Steve.

'Yes.'

'I LOVE blue Mr Freezes.' Steve was enthusiastic about Mr Freezes.

'Then there is no hope for you,' said Syzmon, cracking open another can of cider.

'There probably isn't much hope for anyone,' said Steve. 'The world is a dark and terrible place. But there is blue drink and sometimes there are pirate shanties.'

'What is a shanty?'

'It's like a song. But piratey. They feature rum a lot. And graves. And Davey Jones's locker'

Steve missed Joel a little. She felt all of her secrets bubbling up inside of her, waiting to spill out, and she wasn't sure she wanted them to. Steve looked at Felix, from across the room, the way a stalker would. At his white throat and the black collar of his T-shirt. *Could I spill my secrets all over you?* Steve thought. *It would feel nice but you would hate me after. Or not hate me, but know how weird I was and, like, avoid me.* Steve was a realistic goblin. She had been very sensible, apart from the binge drinking.

The devil cornered Steve upon the stairs. How Steve got from the garden to the stairs is kind of a mystery. The first blank patch in a night that's dipped in bleach.

'Your friend Ciara is trying to score your boyfriend,' stated the devil.

'He's not my boyfriend,' said Steve

'Oh,' said Robb. 'I kind of hoped I was'

Steve smiled at Robb, and then almost fell over.

'If you were my boyfriend, then you wouldn't be kissing Ciara,' she explained.

Robb's bottom lip did that thing where it tenses as though offended. 'I'm not.'

'If you were my boyfriend, then I wouldn't fancy other boys,' Steve offered in what she hoped was an arch manner.

'That's not a thing that happens. You don't, like, flick a switch and stop fancying people just because you're going out with someone. I fancy other people. I fancy her a bit,' said Robb, pointing at the devil.

'No you don't. She is the actual devil. I punched her in her devil face before. And I'd do it again.'

The devil began to weave her way downstairs.

'Really?'

'In a heartbeat. I'm really good at punching people now. Dad gave me lessons. I used to do kissing with Kevin, you know.'

'I didn't know. Kevin with the shell necklace and the girlfriend with the laugh?' Robb said 'shell necklace' the way some people say 'boob job'.

'Yep. Do you know him?'

'We chatted for a bit while I was alphabetising the DVDs. I like to organise things.' He tilted his head to one side like an abandoned puppy. 'Primrose, why did you leave me alone in there?'

'I didn't leave you alone. I was in the garden.'

'I was in the house.'

'But you talked to people. You are a people person. A mixer.'

'I wanted to talk to *you*,' said Robb.

'Why would you want to talk to me?' asked Steve. 'I'm crap.'

And that is when the ink kicks in.

Steve was in the en-suite bathroom at some point.

Someone's legs asked, 'Is she OK?'

Someone put a wet face-cloth on Steve and he was concerned it was going to make him wet the bed as he had misremembered American slumber-party lore in his drunken state.

Robb had his hand around her waist and said things.

Someone asked, 'What happened?'

Steve got up to prove he was OK and then fell over again. *Get up Steve*, he thought. *Get up, get up.*

Steve said to someone, 'I really miss my mum.' Steve said to someone else something about and how when you are really sad, nothing helps you, but when you are medium sad you can get some help and kind of level-up to mostly OK, maybe.

Steve said things to people. People he remembers as being mostly made of legs.

The floor in Syzmon's parents' en-suite bathroom was black and white and really, really clean. *No wonder people hook up in here*, thought Steve. *It surely is a gleaming sex-palace.*

Steve was kissing someone's mouth. She didn't know whose mouth it was but it belonged to someone and was soft and linked her to the world.

Maybe if I keep doing kissing, thought Steve, *I will not want to do any more puking.*

Steve puked more.

And that is the sorry tale of Steve the goblin. I kissed a person. I do not know who the person was. I assume it might have been Robb. Maybe? I puked on my leggings. I puked all over my skirt and leggings. That is why they weren't there. Ciara found them on the floor of the en-suite bathroom. Which we helped tidy up. My brain felt like it had been preserved in something gelid but I Frankenstein's-monstered my way through the clear-up for Syzmon's sake.

Parties are messy. Ciara found a runner in the salad drawer.

'At least it wasn't mine,' I said, smiling at her in a shame-faced manner.

She smiled back at me. I tried to smile back but ended up squinting.

'So what happened with Robb?' asked Steve, and Ciara made a face.

'Don't ask me what happened with Robb,' she said. 'It's kind of humiliating.'

'Hello? I puked on everything and fell over and said things I can only kind of half remember.'

'Nothing you can say will give me cause to judge you,' said Ciara.

'I don't like pink and blue drinks.'

'I don't like ANY drinks. I keep smelling them on cups and having to dry-retch.'

Syzmon came into the room then and Ciara made secret no-talking-about-hitting-on-other-boys eyebrows, which made me think she might not be finished with him yet. I'm kind of glad Robb didn't kiss her.

I wish I fancied Robb more than I do. He seems to like me. No idea why, but he seems to like me. He's even been replying to my texts after he saw me puke. A lot of people saw me puke. Ciara was trying to have me thinking that no-one had at first. I had to quiz her, name by name. Like, ten people saw. And if ten people saw, and each of them told just one person, that is twenty people. Which is a fifth of our year. And our year is a gossipy year. Urgh.

I can't believe I got roaring drunk. I can't believe I did that to myself. I mean, I could have hurt someone, pushed them down the stairs when I stumbled or something. I could have been hurt, fallen and bashed my head or stumbled down into the road or anything. Anything can happen when you don't remember.

I wonder if Brian McAllister remembers killing Mum. I hope he does. I hope it is stuck in his head like a splinter made of pictures and of sounds. I hope it hurts. I hope it really hurts. Like, more than my head hurts now at the moment. At least fifty per cent more. I think if it was any more than fifty per cent more he might die from it. Which

would be good, but he has kids so I don't want him dead.
A kid needs both their parents. If that is what they're used
to, I mean.

When you're properly sick and really have to concentrate on what people are saying and being in the world,
it is kind of how I imagine a ghost feels. You can feel
your attention fuzzing in and out and you know you're
not yourself, you're not yourself, but who else are you if
you're not yourself, who would you be? A paler, sicker
version. Less able. Less interesting. Less. It's not that
much of a jump to make yourself transparent after that.
You have to speak up any time you speak at all when
you feel weak, your voice feels like a croak, red-raw from
what you've done to it, and it takes more effort to be
noticed, listened to.

Syzmon and Ciara homed in on each other as soon
as he came in the room, and they did the washing up.
He washing, she drying and putting away. I'm glad he
doesn't know about her trying to kiss Robb. Which was
kind of cold. I never would have thought of her as cold
before, not Ciara. But she wasn't like she normally is. She
was more and less fun in equal measure. Which goes for
me as well.

I mean, I'd rather not have sung the shanties with
people because I don't want to be that weird girl who
sings shanties even though she's nearly grown. But there
are plenty of ways I humiliate myself sober.

When I was little, the first bra that I had was mostly
duct-tape and I couldn't get it off and had to take shower
after shower and pull at my skin which is tenderer than
skin in other places. Maybe not tenderer, but nervier or

something. Sometimes my boobs really, really hurt for like a day and a half for no reason and someone brushes against me accidentally or bumps their bag into my side or chest and I seriously want to deck them or stamp on their feet and be, 'See how you like it.'

I wasn't worried I'd been raped or anything, when I woke up with no pants. But I was worried that people had seen my down below places, or that I'd strode around half nude bellowing like a calf or something. Which wouldn't be the worst-case scenario, but would definitely be in the top 5. I'm not going to say I'll give up drink because that would be ridiculous and people never, ever stick to that. But I will give up drinking to keep people who are drinking things company, I think. That seems sensible. Lesson learned.

I really feel I've grown or something. And, best of all,

Dad never needs to know.

I met Úna from school today on Grafton Street.

She looked me up and down and exclaimed, 'Oh, you're expecting,' while smiling a smile that could have been painted on by an artist who specialises in portraits of affected little creeps. I hate telling people for the first time. She's going to be a barrister. 'When the baby comes, I'll have to come and see it,' she said. Little does she know that when the baby comes, I am going to teach it to hate her. Which might sound cold, but I have so few pleasures in my life and need to take what I can get.

o, I crawled in home like a slug. Literally, like a slug. Ciara's mum was going to buy us lunch and even the *word* 'lunch' made my toes turn grey and the grey was spreading up into my face and Ciara sensed it and said, 'No, no. We ate earlier.'

Quote from Prim's mum's diary

Even though I know she was pure hungry because her tummy rumbled all the way in the car to my house and her mum was all, 'Are you sure you aren't hungry?' and suspicious but Ciara covered it up, saying that she just had got indigestion from all the food she'd eaten. Which, as far as thinking on your eet goes, is kind of brilliant.

Robb texted again, to ask how I was, which was nice of him, but I'm kind of too embarrassed to reply. Was he the legs? Who were the legs? And were they all one set of legs or was it several legs belonging to different people?

There was definitely one unfriendly set there anyway, because although I had no recollection of Karen being anywhere near me at the end of the night, Dad had received a text from her mother's phone containing video footage of me puking into a shower tray. I'm not saying anything too bad, but my legs are bare and there is a boy in the room and that is enough to convince the Daddy-man that I am one sperm short of a pregnancy.

I hate Karen. Dad hates her too and thinks that it was very unfair that she sent him the video. But he has to punish me now that he has evidence. I asked him if I could take a nap first, and he said I could. But once I wake up, I will find out what my punishment will be for underage drinking to excess and lying about where I was and things. He copped right away that I couldn't have stayed in Ciara's.

'Because Ciara still had hair left on her scalp when she dropped you off, and Nóirín would have had it dragged off of her, if she'd got even a whiff of drink.'

This was how he put it. In fairness, he is not wrong. I am in so much trouble.

I still have ghost-feelings all through my body. Like I'm a series of images and memories and not a person. Like I am made of wisps of fatigue and woe. I'm dying to nod off, but it's hard knowing I'll wake up and be punished. I wonder how Mary Queen of Scots slept, or Anne Boleyn, the nights before they were due to be executed. My pillow is really soft. I think Dad changed the sheets for me this morning. It smells nice here, more homey than at Syzmon's.

When I moved here first, it smelled new and old at the same time. So different to the home I'd had with Mum. The little crooked stairs up to our flat. The baking press and glass jars with candles in. The candles Dad has come in jars already. And when the candle's burnt, he throws the jar out with it, as if it couldn't be re-used. I save them sometimes. Put ribbons and jewellery in them. I suppose when you're a man you don't need pretty jars as much. You've got fewer bits. He could put his ties in a jar, I suppose, but the little hanger especially for them he has is probably better in the long run. Moustache combs! That's what he could put in them. He has a few, because he keeps losing them. He could put the jar of moustache combs on the back of the toilet and he'd never be lost for one again. They'd have a place.

I must tell him that idea when I wake up. Either before or after he exiles me, or whatever half-assed punishment he thinks of. He might send me to some actual salt-mines. I bet he could and all. He's got connections. I need to sleep. I need to go to sleep.

Oh, brain, why won't you let me go to sleep? I need a break from being me. Just for a couple of hours. I hope it's dreamless. I feel like I am far too tired for dreams.

Z

z

z

My stomach is huge. It's impossibly huge. If I were wearing big clown shoes, I still wouldn't be able to see my feet. I think the baby will come soon. I'm not quite at my due date, but I feel like a microwave that's just about to ping. Come get me, doctors, I'm done with this. It's cooked.

TEXTS I HAVE GOT SINCE THE PARTY:

CIARA:

Was it weird that I tried to hook up with Robb? It was weird, wasn't it? It was weird! I'm sorry. Let's never speak of it again. ☺

Quote from Prim's mum's diary

JOEL:

Hey. So I hear you got wasted and puked everywhere. I shouldn't have to hear that stuff from Karen, Prim. You should tell me all your embarrassing things first. So I can be supportive and also make fun of you. 😊 Also, I might have mildly lost some of my virginity. Exciting times.

CIARA:

What happened was, I went in for the kiss with him and he moved his head away and I got his cheek and he was all, 'I'm kind of with your friend, what are you doing?' and I said that you were fine with it and he said, 'You *talked* about this?' and then he looked a bit sad but I still tried to hook up with him again because I am a single-minded drunk and he did the cheek thing again and now I can't even think about him without feeling terribly embarrassed and ashamed and sort of like a predator.

CIARA:

What are you doing? he asked, What are you doing? Oh, God. WHAT WAS I DOING?

JOEL:

We'll talk in person about it. But you have to promise not to get all judgey and ask leading questions that imply that he is taking advantage of me.

JOEL:

I know you can't help doing that. But you can't blame me for trying to stop you. I might be in love with him, Prim. Sometimes it dances up into my mouth and I have to swallow it down, because I'm scared that if I say it, it will change EVERYTHING.

ROBB:

Do you want to meet up next week? x

ROBB:

That sounds cool – but you have to show up. You can't, like, pimp me out to one of your friends or anything. x

FELIX:

Are you all right? How's the head? ☺

ELLA:

What happened at the party? You were normal, a bit expressive, but normal. But Felix told me things about puking on and in things and it makes me worry. Did you get food poisoning or were you just drunk?

ELLA:

Oh. You probably shouldn't drink any more, then. We can be sober together. Like a club. Felix saw you get sick all right. He got a bit on his runners, but you mostly puked on Robb with two bees, apparently. Felix thinks he's sound. They were talking about music and things while you were vomming in the shower tray.

JOEL:

I'll come over to your house and we'll watch a movie. I don't want to talk about underage sexing in a public place. In case Duncan gets arrested or my mum finds out.

JOEL:

He SHOULD NOT get arrested, Prim. God, sometimes I wonder why I tell you stuff at all. Maybe you should be arrested for underage drinking and wilful destruction of property.

JOEL:

Loads of people's shoes, apparently.

FELIX:

Don't worry about it. I got most of it out with a toothbrush. It makes them a bit more rock and roll or something. Probably.

ROBB:

They were not my only pair of shoes, Prim. Do you want to go see the Deep Tinkers play on Thursday? x

ROBB:

Oh. I'm sorry. Who told your dad? x

ROBB:

Who is she again? The one with the Aspergers or the one who is the devil? x

NORA:

Are you OK? Karen texted me to tell me you'd made a complete fool of yourself. Which you totally didn't. Because I've seen worse. I've seen her be worse.

ELLA:

You are a nice person. Are you coming to see Felix play on Thursday? Caleb is coming with me.

ELLA:

I know. I would hate if Felix were in prison. But he doesn't really break the law.

SYZMON:

How is the head? Don't worry about it. It is what happens when there is a party. I've been that guy before. Everyone has been that guy.

SYZMON:

Did Ciara say anything about me?

CIARA:

I don't know. Why is he asking you?

CIARA:

OK, you can tell him I said that I really like him as a friend and that I miss spending time with him.

CIARA:

Do NOT tell him about Robb. I don't want anyone to know.

KEVIN:

How's the head?

KEVIN:

I wasn't being mean. I am genuinely concerned for your head.

KEVIN:

We didn't kiss. I have a girlfriend, Prim. Jesus.

KEVIN:

Siobhán's here with me right now. She knows I'm texting you.

SIOBHÁN:

Hi, Prim. I'm sorry you made a fool of yourself on Saturday. These things happen, though. Kevin gave me your number. I know he was texting you. We tell each other everything.

JOEL:

WHAT. A. TOOLBAG.

CIARA:

Can't believe that. She was always odd, though. Even when I was friends with her. She'll turn on him. Mark my words.

ELLA:

Ugh. That text would make me feel sad. Did it make you feel sad? I am going to glare at Siobhán next time I see her. I'd offer to have Mr Cat attack Wayne Rooney but it isn't Kevin's dog's fault his owner is an idiot.

CIARA:

It's very unhealthy to be so co-dependent early on. Maybe they'll become serial killers together.

CIARA:

I miss Syzmon. (Don't tell him I said that.)

SYZMON:

So, what you are saying is I should not give up all hope? ☺

JOEL:

Karen tagged you in a photograph. She must have unblocked you. You are clearly going to be besties now.

JOEL:

Oh, sorry. I didn't look at it properly. You should report her for that. They'll take it down. Have you untagged yourself?

CIARA:

It's just one of your legs. No-one will know it's you anyway.

CIARA:

I hate her too, sweetheart.

CIARA:

Did you talk to your dad yet?

CIARA:

Stop pretending to be asleep and go and talk to him.

CIARA:

Like pulling off a bandage.

CIARA:

Go Team!

CIARA:

Is he gonna tell Mam about the drinking? ☺

ROBB:

I don't care about Lion Tamarind Monkeys, Prim. How are you keeping? X

DOLPHIN LAURA:

How's the head? Heard you had a bit of a late one!!

DOLPHIN LAURA:

Well, I certainly didn't notice any foolish behaviour. What did u get up 2, you scamp? ☺

DOLPHIN LAURA:

We've all been there.

ROBB:

We didn't kiss. I like to kiss you when you know it's me. x

ROBB:

I don't like monkeys at all actually. Their wise little faces unnerve me. x

ROBB:

Please stop. Monkeys shouldn't be orange. Brown is the colour they're supposed to be. x

ROBB:

Why are you doing this? x

ROBB:

Is it a weird form of flirting? x

ROBB:

Because I don't think monkeys are sexy and if you
do, I think we'll have a problem. x

ROBB:

OMG Prim, stop. I'll turn off my phone. x

ROBB:

I will tell you dreadful things about otters if you
don't stop. X

I thought that once you were in labour things would go quickly. That it would be 'BOOM, pain, swearing, baby.' But no. I am walking around waiting for my cervix to dilate. I have been OK with not having a dilated cervix for all of my life up till now. Dilation was for pupils when I looked at Fintan or biscuits.

Less so at Fintan these days. He is being very unsupportive. Biscuits are probably a better bet.

Dad is banning me from all things that could have drink at them for three months. This includes dancey things, house parties, Junior Cert results night and cinema after 7PM unless I am accompanied by an adult chaperone.

'That's ridiculous.'

'Less ridiculous than puking all over your friend's house.'

Quote from Prim's mum's diary

197

'Yes.'

'Really?'

'No. But it is unfair.' I frowned at him.

'More unfair than lying about where you are staying at night to your aging father?' He was enjoying this a bit too much.

'You aren't that aging.'

'I'm more aged than you. And that means I know some things about the way the world works. Let me break it down for you. I am the adult. So I have the money and the authority and the power. You are the child, so you have none of these things unless I give them to you. Which I often choose to do, because you are my daughter and I love you. But, at the end of the day, Prim, what I say goes.'

'You never told me not to drink,' I pointed out.

'I asked you whether there would be drink there, and you told me that there would be but it wouldn't be your drink.'

'That much was true, though.'

'Whose drink was it, so?' he asked.

'People's.'

'So you were going around stealing other people's drink all night?'

'No.'

'Then it was your drink. I don't care who actually bought it or brought it. What I care about is whose gullet it went down.'

'Gross.'

'What?'

'GULLET.'

'I've booked an appointment with Caroline and informed her about this debacle. And –'

'And you will be going every week for the next four weeks. Longer if she thinks you need it. I am not letting you develop a drinking problem.'

'I am **NOT** developing a drinking problem, Dad.'

'You denied the cutting thing too. But I've seen the scars on your legs and stomach.'

'When were you looking at my stomach? Jesus.'

'I'm going for dinner with Sorrel tonight. And I've asked Mary if you can stay at her house.'

'And be, like, minded? I'm not a baby, Dad.'

'If you want to be treated like a grown-up, you can start acting like one.'

'Some grown-ups get drunk,' I muttered.

'Well, they don't puke all over their friends' houses and get filmed doing it.'

'I bet some of them do.'

'You've got a very smart mouth, haven't ya?' he went pure country on that last bit. When Dad goes country you know he's really irked.

Smart?

'I'm sorry, Dad,' I said.

And I kind of meant it. He looked all worried. And I did feel bad about making an idiot of myself. Not that I think I did anything wrong, apart from drink too much. I mean, everyone lies to their parents. It's like a big part of being a teenager is lying to other people about what you do and how you think and how you feel. It might be a big part of being an adult too, for all I know. Loads of adults lie. Dad lied to Mum. He said he loved her. And that they were going to get married. And look how that turned out.

'Yes, well. You're lucky all that happened is you threw up a bit. Girls have to be careful you know. Someone could have taken advantage of you.' Had someone told him about the no-pants thing? They couldn't have. I mean, I'm still alive.

'At Syzmon's party?'

'If you'd lost your friends. Bad things can happen any-where, Prim. No matter how safe you feel, you're never fully safe. And if you're drunk, you're way more vulner-able. You need to keep your eyes open to the world around you.'

'I do, Dad. I'm normally very careful. I've never got like that before. It was ... it was scary. I didn't like it and I feel terrible.'

'OK. Well, we've discussed it now. So all you have to do is take your punishment and we'll say no more about it.'

He totally will say more about it, though. I know my dad: he won't be able to help himself. It'll eat away at him, how right he was. How much moral high ground he gained and, next time he needs to crawl back up there, he'll use that night to make his point more pointy. Sharper. Not that I really blame him. I mean, I'd do it too. If I were in his fancy leather shoes.

I'd like to live in a world where people didn't gather ammunition on each other. Sadly, that world would only contain me and perhaps a companion animal. Maybe a chinchilla. Chinchillas seem like gentle little dudes. It'd need to be pretty live-and-let-live to be on my island and put up with me. If there were even one other person there, though, there would be gathering. Hunting for ammo, gathering it up and using it to hurt a person later or to make their little point. Sometimes I wish I weren't even human. I wish I were a soft, peaceable thing. Like a chinchilla or a guinea-pig. I could be gentler then, if I didn't have this big a brain. If I were mostly made of soul and instinct.

Who did I kiss? I really wish I could remember. Was it Felix? There's no way it could have been him, right?

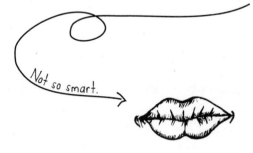

Not so smart.

Sorrel came in on her lunch break to keep me company and when she saw that Fintan wasn't there and I was frightened, she stayed with me. My waters broke and I had that mucous thing and it was pink, which was really weird because I'd always envisioned mucus as either clear or white or green or yellow. Those were the acceptable colours for it. I walked around and she held my hand and I obsessed over whether or not she was going to get fired and she said, 'A new life is coming out of you, 'Bláth,' and 'That is so far from being the most important thing you could be thinking about.' She rubbed my back. The doctors said it might relieve the pain. It didn't really, but I still liked getting rubbed.

Dad's date with Sorrel went quite well I think. And it wasn't the worst thing in the world to get sent to Ella's house. It's just I'd like to visit her out of friendship,

Quote from Prim's mum's diary

202

not because I have to be babysat in case my nascent drinking problem escalates further. Mary had obviously heard about the incident. She did the eyebrows at me and made a few pointed little comments. In a good-natured way. Which still kind of made me feel embarrassed and frustrated.

Felix was more sympathetic. 'I can't believe Karen did that. I mean, not that I can't believe she would do that because she clearly would and did and all. But she was really subtle. I hardly noticed her there, and she certainly wasn't brandishing her phone or anything.'

'She's a smooth operator, that one,' said Mary, who was popping in and out of the kitchen as we drank our tea. Probably to make sure I didn't offer Felix a feed of pints and then try it on with him.

'She is,' said Ella. 'I wish I'd been there.'

'No, you don't.'

'Yes, I do. I've never seen anyone be that drunk before. Except for Felix's Junior Cert results night.'

'Shut up, Ella,' said Felix.

'I won't. Hearing about other people's mistakes will make Prim feel better. He had a naggin and then drank some more things as well and then fell over and Mum had to come to the crap youth disco thing they organise every year to collect him.'

'What was it called that year?' I asked.

Felix smiled ruefully. 'Junior Jams.'

'Oh God. I wonder what they'll call it this year. Not that I'll be going.'

'They could call it Cert du Soleil,' offered Felix.

'Or Sexy Results.'

'Too far. I wonder if we'll all go anyway, without you.' Ella was running her fingers through her hair, ratting out the little tangles.

'I expect you will,' I said, feeling sorry for myself.

'I mightn't,' said Ella. 'It depends on how awkward things get with Caleb.'

'When do the Leaving Cert results come out, Felix?'

'Oh, way before the junior ones. Middle of August, so we've another two weeks to go.'

'Are you nervous?'

'Not really.' He swallowed. 'A bit. I mean, the points for sound engineering aren't that high. Science is higher, but I kind of only put that down for Mum.'

'A diploma is not a degree.' Felix's mum was folding towels and putting them in drawers.

'I can get a *job* out of it, Mum. A job I'll actually like.' Felix looked a tired kind of angry.

'How did Karen get your dad's number anyway?' asked Ella

'Her mum had it from back when I was homophobic-bullying her and Dad and her parents had to have meetings and things.'

I made air quotes with my voice for 'homophobic bullying'. It still stings that people think of me as a bully. I only hate gay people who are Karen. And Karen doesn't even seem to be that gay any more, so maybe that puts me in the clear. Or maybe people will think I have scared her back into the lady closet. At least Nora doesn't hate me any more. Which is good, because I think I have been sufficiently hated for one year.

Felix and Ella and I made dinner together. It was lasagne and baked potatoes and garlic bread. The lasagne was pre-made by Mary but we still had to do the washing-up. It was kind of nice. I wondered what it would be like to have a brother or a sister close in age to me. Someone to help and be helped by. I think it would be nice.

We all curled up on the sofa after dinner and watched a nature documentary about wolves. I shared some rather interesting facts with Robb.

> How are you? X

I began, to lure him in.

> Not too bad, now. What are you up to? X

The true answer was, 'Being minded in Ella's house in case I turn to heroin while my Dad goes on a date with my dead mother's best friend and also I fancy Ella's brother, Felix, who you met on the night of Syzmon's party when I threw up on your shoes and basically offered you to my friend for kissing purposes like I was an aging warlord and you were my beautiful young courtesan. Oh dear God.' So I opted instead for:

> Not much. Eurasian wolves tend to be more adaptable than North American wolves in the face of human expansion. X

> Not this again. X

> They have coarser fur than their yank cousins also. X

So does your mother. X

My mother is dead, Robb. One of the largest
Eurasian wolves on record weighed 189 lbs. X

He rang me as soon as he got that. He was all stumbling and sorrying and I could tell he thought he'd really put his foot in it. But, to be honest, it was kind of a relief that he forgot. Like, it wasn't the most important thing about me. Like, he doesn't fancy me because he feels sorry for me. It was nice.

I texted him to let him know that wolves were a huge part of Ireland's postglacial fauna. I think he knew that meant that things were OK.

It's weird to think of Ireland under ice. Like Snow White in a coffin, waiting to wake up and be a living breathing bit of world again. A world with wolves inside. A world with ringforts.

Dad picked me up and when I asked him how his date had been he said OK and then went straight to bed. Maybe she unleashed her crazy on him. Sorrel has a wealth of benign crazy. She owns like seven scrying crystals. I'm still not sure how to feel about two people, both of whom I want to see happy, being together in that way. I mean, it is gross to think about Dad having a romantic life. That's just a given. But I've seen him mess around so many women, and I've seen Sorrel on both sides of romantic messes. They knew each other way back when, and that is kind of difficult, you see, because they have so much ammunition. And Mum can't not be hanging there between them, like a spectre. I wish she were a spectre. We could hang out. She could give me guidance and things. Maybe we could even solve some mysteries together. Or she could get to know the me I am today, instead of the child I was. I mean, there are a lot of things the same about me. But also a lot different. I have new friends and hair and like new music. I fancy boys and sometimes even kiss them. I think about sex. And not like it's a thing that grown-ups do. Like it's a thing that I might one day do. That I am curious about. I probably wouldn't tell that to ghost-Mum, but I could ask her certain questions about boys and girls and life and things.

Mum wasn't judgemental. She was a great listener. I can imagine her haunting me. The night of my debs, putting on mascara and I'd get a whiff of her orangey-lilac perfume and I'd turn and there'd be no-one there. But when I turned back to the mirror she'd be in there behind me, her hand stroking my hair and looking proud. She'd mouth, 'I love you Primmy,' or, 'I love you Pose,' and then she'd fade but I'd know she was there, still watching and caring.

I don't think there's an afterlife at all. And I think the reason I still turn it over in my mind and question it is because I want there to be one so badly. I want the end of things to not be the end of all things ever. But only of corporeal things. I want the spirits, live and shimmering somewhere fabulous, to linger and reach out towards our world and maybe touch. Ghost Mum. Ghost Roderick. Ghost Granny and Grandads. I didn't really know them, though, so while I'd like to have had the chance to know them properly, like Ciara did Lily, I don't feel the lack of them, pulling at my stomach in the night. Missing them never stops me sleeping.

Red bumpy lines turn to purple bumpy lines turn to pink bumpy lines. I haven't thought about cutting myself in ages. And I'm not thinking about it now. I'm just smoothing myself. Taking stock. Accounting. Everything's in ledgers in accounting. Debit. Credit. Dad says it's a life-skill. He wants me to take it for the Leaving. I don't really like it. Do I need it? I wonder if all my sins and kindnesses would balance. If there was a heaven – and there's not – but say there was a heaven, would I get in or just be left behind? I don't think that I'd go to hell, not really. But I could be left. That would loop in nicely to my life. Would snugly fit.

Everyone is always leaving me behind. It's a good thing I like my own company. A blessing. I don't feel blessed, though, endowed with special favour by the gods. Can you be blessed if you don't have a god? You can probably be lucky? I wonder if everyone who's lucky believes in God. If you made a graph of that, it would be interesting.

No, it wouldn't. Why does Dad not want to talk to me?

He arrived and I dilated. Those two things are COMPLETELY unrelated. 'Holding on for Daddy,' the doctor said, and Fintan gave an 'Aww'. I gave a snort. I am mad at him. And in a good deal of pain. 'What are you writing?' he wants to know. I glare at him. SELFISH MAN is what I'm writing.

Fintan. Guess who it applies to?

Dad sat me down to have a talk with me this morning. He did that thing – you know, in books, when someone clears their throat and it's written as 'HARRUMPH'? Well, he basically cleared his throat but also said

'HARRUMPH'

Quote from Prim's mum's diary

'Did you just say "HARRUMPH"?' He had. But I wanted to make sure.

'I did, yes. I was about to tell you something.' He cleared his throat again, but in a less showy manner.

'What?'

'Well, I have something to tell you.'

'What sort of something?' I asked.

'Something big. I'm not sure how to broach it with you, really ... I mean ...'

His face went a bit pale and all his features contracted a little. My heart began to eat itself.

'Are you dying, Dad?'

'No.'

'Because you have to tell me if you're dying. Like, as soon as you know yourself, you have to tell me. It's like a rule.'

I was pretty close to crying at this stage. I had him gone through a range of unsuccessful treatments, wasting, dead and buried.

'There is no such rule. Dying people are above rules.'

'No, they aren't. They have to tell their daughters right away. And also not die. Is it bowel cancer?'

'What? No.'

'Testicular.' I nodded. I had read things on the Internet about older men, letting their scrotal lumps go by unnoticed. 'You really should get regular checks at your age.'

'I don't have testicular cancer, Prim. I don't have any type of cancer at all. I am healthy. Very healthy. It's just. I want to tell you something else. Something positive. Something good, in fact. A surprise. A lovely surprise.' He was poking at his nail beds and smiling without blinking.

'What is it?'

'Um.'

'Dad!'

'WE'RE GOING ON A HOLIDAY!' he exclaimed, as though he were a chat-show host and I a studio audience.

'Oh.' This *was* a surprise. Were we going to Paris?

'A lovely holiday.' He nodded his head, agreeing with himself.

'And you're sure you're not dying? Of any type of cancer or heart disease or any type of older human male thing?'

'I am definitely not dying, Prim.'

'Because the way you've presented this holiday to me feels an awful lot like a sort of a consolation prize for bad news.'

'I don't give consolation prizes for bad news.'

'You TOTALLY do. You gave me a new phone when Roderick died,' I pointed out.

'That's, like, *one* time. And it was your birthday.'

'When you mess up, you always get me stuff. Like caramel squares or vouchers that you get in fancy work hampers and never use.' (I love backing things up with evidence. It's like a super-power everyone can have, All you need are FACTS.)

'I'll stop,' said Dad.

'Don't – it's kind of nice. A blow-softener, if you will.'

'I won't.'

'HA.'

Sometimes, when people say things that don't make me actually laugh, but are funny none the less, I find myself actually saying 'ha'. Ha is my harrumph. My real laughter cannot be transcribed phonetically. It's a kind of soft cackle that gets increasingly brittle as it escalates. Ciara and I and Joel sometimes cackle in tandem and it is a beautiful thing indeed. A beautiful, ugly thing as our laughter blends to make sounds that no human thing should make at all. The sound of ridiculous, helpless laughter makes things funnier. It amplifies the fun and sucks your agency, until you are a collection of wobbles and nerve endings. Mum had a ridiculous laugh as well, the kind of laugh that you would hear and laugh at.

But, in fairness, Dad's retort was not that funny. So I just said 'HA' and left it at that.

We are going to London. Which isn't that far away. And it is a bit of a business trip as well. But the good thing is because it is a business trip, and Dad won't be around all the time, he is going to see if Joel can come over for a few days too, and be my holiday friend. If Joel can't come he'll ask Ciara. Isn't it funny that he assumed that's where my preferences lay, and I suppose they do lie there traditionally speaking, but Joel being cold to me for so long has kind of brought me and Ciara closer and also made me aware that Joel can do that. Turn his back on thirteen years of friendship for an idea that he'll later admit was wrong and a backlog of unimportant slights.

I know the Kevin thing was important at the time, it was. But now it's water under the bridge. Horrible, sewagey water that should not be allowed to dally with girls again until it has had some hardcore sensitivity training.

I've been to London once before, with Mum. We went to see a ballet of *The Secret Garden*. It was one of Mum's favourite books when she was a little girl and she read it to me and then I read it by myself and it was one of my favourites too. We couldn't often afford big holidays, like the kids in my class had. Mum couldn't pay and I don't think it ever occurred to Dad that I would like to go abroad with him. I'd like to go to Spain some time. Spain is such a normal place to have visited, but I've never been. I've only been to places Mum had friends that she could stay with. Berlin. Vienna. London. Belfast. Meath. Dad and I are going to be staying in a big hotel. And I'm going to have my own room. There'll be, like, a door between the two so he can keep an eye on my drinking, but that's still very cool in my book.

Dad drove me to my Caroline appointment. I was texting Robb about Bengal tigers for a bit. It's not that I fancy Robb *per se*. But I have been turning him over in my mind like he was a peculiarly shaped piece of stone I'd picked up on the beach. Maybe a denim-coloured limestone with marble bits striated in. Or granite. I think he'd make a very handsome quartzy granite pebble. I think about him at the oddest times. Like, with Felix, I'm always thinking of things that I could do to impress him.

1.

Become a world-class musician.

2.

Become a beauty, in a cool indie-music magazine kind of way. The kind of beauty that's always a millimetre away from having a face on her. Dark hair. Pale skin. Red lips. Possible vampirism.

3.

Offer to sleep with him.

I don't think number three would actually impress him, as it would be very desperate and creepy of me. But he is a teenage boy who hasn't had a girlfriend in a year and a half, so maybe he thinks about sex. And I am a girl, so sex is technically something he could have with me. If he wanted to. He totally wouldn't, though. I think he'd think that he was taking advantage of me or some such nonsense. When in reality, it would be the other way around. OH-HO.

Anyway, recently, like since the party, when Ciara wanted him, I think Robb has been entering into my maniacal thought-patterns. He is a bit easier to impress than Felix. I think number three would probably appeal to him, but obviously, he's not going to get near that level of intimacy until I'm good and sure I fancy him. By which time he'll have gone back to his wonderful boarding school where everything is peachy keen and forgotten all about me. Oh my God, I'M HIS SUMMER GIRLFRIEND. As Caleb is to Ella, so am I to Robb. It's like those word association things Ms Griffin sometimes gives out in CSPE.

I hate CSPE. It seems like a doss subject, but then it isn't and so you only do half-assed work for it and find yourself struggling during revision week because everything that was said in class got filtered out.

I could impress Robb by:

1.

Trolling him with animal facts.

2.

Kissing him and smelling his neck.

3.

Offering to sleep with him.

4.

Solving a notable mystery.

5.

Being a boarding school.

Numbers one and two are the easiest. I think a combo of them and number four would be amazing. I know he likes me fine right now and that is positive. And it isn't that I want to marry him or anything, I'm just worried he'll find out the kind of person I am and change his mind. Because people do change their minds all the time in relationships.

Caroline was asking me about the party. She got me to tell it to her, and I had to go back through everything again, only with me playing the Steve role, because I don't want to be, like, committed or anything. I wonder can a therapist have someone committed? She is a doctor as well as a cognitive behavioural therapist. I mean, she has her medical degree up on her wall. I can see the grain of the paper and I think it is unlikely that she just printed up a fake one off the Internet to impress her patients. I don't think it'd be legal for one thing. So maybe Caroline could have me committed if she wanted to. I wonder what it would take. Like, a suicide attempt? Or maybe hearing voices? People with schizophrenia do that sometimes. Hear things that aren't really there. Only they sound as if they are there, right in their ear. Telling them things. And when something seems that real, it's hard to know who to listen to. Sometimes I worry about my brain. All the stuff I've gone through since Mum's death has made me aware of all that can go wrong.

Before Mum died, I thought of illness as a body thing. Like cancer or pneumonia or a broken leg. Some of them kill you, some of them get cured. But now there's this whole other side. Your brain can get broken and if it's only cracked a little, you can try to fix it yourself. But you mightn't have the tools to do that or, because there is a crack in your brain, you mightn't be able to recognise what the tools you should be using are. And so you try things that aren't helpful. Like I did with the cutting. Some people make themselves sick or don't eat or take drugs or have ill-advised sex in nightclub toilets.

There is a whole slew of things you can do to try to fix yourself that actually sand the edges of the crack, so it feels less broken, smoother but actually it's getting bigger, bigger all the time, and if it gets too big you might die from how big it is, how insurmountable the space between one side of the crack and the other has become. If the crack is big, you mightn't be able to help doing dangerous things. They might seem increasingly sensible, given the circumstances. People kill themselves. They are alive and then they aren't any more, and that's a choice they've made, a desperate lonely choice. To destroy themselves because it genuinely seems like the most sensible option, given how unfixable things have become; how full of sad or angry or both they are.

I think it is yourself that makes you decide to kill yourself. Because not everybody likes themselves, but some people actually hate themselves, hate themselves the way I hate Karen, or the drunk man who killed Mum. More even. I don't want either of them dead. I just don't want them near me. But if you hate you that much, and have to be near yourself all the time, then maybe you would start to hate yourself more and even more until you'd kill yourself.

I think about it sometimes. I used to do way more. But I don't hate myself enough, I think. There's always, like, this little chink of hope. I'm never empty. Mostly I was just tired. I wanted a break from all the life I had. Because it is exhausting, living when you're sad all the

time. You get so little out of it. I'm glad I'm better now.
I mean, I still have my moments. But they don't expand
and bleed into the other moments, until it's rarer to be
happy than sad. Sad is not my normal now. And I don't
think that's completely because of Caroline. A lot of it's
to do with me, and growing up and getting used to things.
Things like hormones. And mothers being dead.

Not that, were she around, she'd have fixed everything. But I wonder how much of it would have been
broken to begin with. Caroline makes me think things
sometimes. After I leave her office, I get all introspective
and walk around, listening to music and formulating
thoughts like they were potions. Trying to decide what I
think. Because a lot of the time I don't know. She said I
could always just drink Diet Coke and say that it was
vodka and Diet Coke, if I felt weird about not drinking. I
kind of don't, though. That's not what it was. I'm comfortable enough to say no to things, but I might have forgotten
to be for a while. Or just forgotten that drinks weren't
sweets, that you can't gorge on them and know that it's
unhealthy but think that they have no real side-effects.

I have to make a list of things I do. Like, activities each
day. She wants my weekly leisure time-table to analyse.
Or written out, for me to analyse myself while she listens
and judges in a way that seems like she isn't judging. But

she is, she totally is. I mean, everyone makes judgements about everyone else all the time. We can't help it. We're human. It's our thing.

I have a funny feeling about this holiday. Like somehow there is something more to it. I don't think he has cancer, but I've got the weirdest niggle, not in the pit of my stomach but kind of in the corner of the pit. And the niggle is telling me that Dad is, if not up to something, at least not telling me the full story. But it's a week in London, so what mystery can there be, really?

I already know he'll have to work for some of it, so that's out there. I don't know. I'm probably being over-analytical. The scar where my brain-crack used to be sometimes lets a bit (or a lot) of negative spill out all over a day or a person or an interaction.

But what's the deal with London? We're leaving in three days. It seems quite sudden. My pit-niggle is shaped like a question mark but there's very little I can do about it.

I wonder if I'll get to see Robb before I leave. I've been turning it over in my mind. The night of the party. When he didn't want to kiss Ciara. Just me. His pillow-mouth. His eyes. I think I'd like to. I think looking at him might make things in my head stay put or fall apart, like sexual attraction Jenga.

'My little girl is here. She is a human being. She has eyes. They're shiny and they blink. I can't stop looking at her. Everything about her is so perfect. I'm going to do my best for you, I'm thinking as I look at her. I'm going to try so hard to make you happy. She looks like herself already. I mean, she looks like Winston Churchill after he's gone through a hot-cycle wash as well, but she has features that don't belong to me or Fintan. They're all her own. At 0 years of age.

Joel is coming to London!! He'll be there for the first three days and then we'll put him on the plane home and Dad and me will hang out. I'm so excited. He's coming over at some point soon to plan and also tell me the story of what happened with him and Duncan the night of the party. I'm pretty interested to find out.

Quote from Prim's mum's diary

≡ 221 ≡

I mean, I don't want an enormous level of detail. Probably. But I haven't had someone like he has Duncan yet, a friend like that. And even though Duncan is a gross disgusting older dude and whatnot, he is cute and he is into Joel. Which are both good qualities in a boyfriend.

Apparently Anne and Liam want Joel to come to London with us because he's been spending far too much of his summer going out. I wish I'd been invited to all these going-outs. It's weird to think of someone you used to do everything with having their own life and stuff. I'm not sure that I like it. Who told Joel he was allowed to have a social life that didn't involve me?

I wonder what Duncan's circle are like. Joel says they're nice. Older, like college age and over, but nice and friendly and they don't make him feel like he's a child or anything. I'd feel pure awkward there, if I was invited, I reckon. And he'd need to mind me, keep me company. And sitting beside a sixteen-year-old girl would only highlight how young he was, and he'd hate that. He's been doing subtle things to look older. Sometimes he wears ties. It doesn't really work. I mean, you can't change what age you are. Just because you both bought the same satchel in Topman doesn't mean you're equally mature.

I've only met Duncan three times. Which is fine, and he's been nice on each occasion, but anyone can be nice three times. That's not, like, *challenging*. And there's a huge bit of me that feels like to get to have a relationship with someone as interesting and as cool and as wonderful and as everything as Joel, you should have to undergo at the very least a rigorous interview process. And I think I am the person best qualified to hold said interviews. And

Duncan seems to have slipped in to Joel's life in spite of our friendship, without my say, without my being there at any level in the early stages. Which was partially my own fault for being a tool in my dealings with Karen, but if Joel were going to stop talking to me every time I acted like a tool then we would probably not have been best friends in the first place.

And we were, and we are. And I'm really glad we are. I love my Joel. I wish his brother Marcus were older, so I could discuss the Duncan thing with him. Take him for tea and make fun of him for the year and a half where he dressed like a robot almost constantly and then be all, 'Marcus? What do you think about the moderately sized man your brother may or may not have already done grown-up things with?'

I don't think I could ever say that sentence out loud. It would probably have a detrimental effect on Marcus to think about Joel and sexy-time in the same sentence. I don't even like thinking about it and I have been known to read slash fiction from time to time to while away the twilight hours.

I got a text from Sorrel today as well.

Has your father told you the good news? ☺

Yeah, really excited. Never been to London before. How did the date go? ☺

She didn't reply to me. It's weird, because she's normally quite quick to. I mean, she's scatty as anything but she's kind of the closest I have to an aunty.

Looking at my baby girl. At her little tummy poking out above the nappy. Her bellybutton's got a little clamp thing on it. She still has a bit of umbilical cord. But as she grows it will shrivel and fall away and she'll have lost the last little bit of me in her and just be all herself. The doctor said that some people choose to keep it. I don't think I'll be one of them.

Hey Robb, you about later on? The Bengal tiger is the most numerous tiger subspecies. So when you think of tigers, you are actually thinking about Bengal tigers. X

I am not. I am thinking about white tigers. Pointedly. X

Ha! The white tiger is a recessive mutant of the Bengal tiger. X

You're a recessive mutant of … your face. I would love to hang out. Aren't you grounded though? X

Quote from Prim's mum's diary

You could call over. But you have to promise not to say anything mean about my face from now on. X

I wasn't being mean. I like your face. You know that. Bengal tigers! X

Their basic social unit is that of one mother and offspring. Adults only interact on a transitory basis. X

Dry. X

Bengal tigers are not dry, Robb. X

They are too. They're no craic. X

I'm no craic. X

You're loads of craic. Big fun head on you. Mam'll drop me over around seven, if that's OK? X

It is OK. Bengal tigers have been known to prey on leopards and bears. X

They have not. I take back what I said about them being no craic. X

I like the way he always replies to my texts, even when they don't have a question in. I like an awful lot about Robb with two bees as a matter of fact. But I wonder if

I'm thinking about him because he fancies me, rather than actually fancying him in his own right. Because, until recently, he used to really bug me. I want to meet him in person again, so I can see if I like him when he's not just a series of responses on my phone.

Joel has cancelled our movie night because he has to spend as much time as possible with Duncan before he goes to London for three nights. He is being very cagey about their recent activities. He does not text details or offer them over the phone. It's like he wanted me to know it happened, but also wanted to keep everything private and that is confusing. Not that I want detailsy details. But I wouldn't mind doing a little bit of analysis, in case he has any pointers for me when I decide to lose my virginity at the age of forty-seven to a man I have hired for the express purpose. AND I'll pathetically fall in love with him and keep paying him to sleep with me and go into hock and then do some credit card fraud and go into prison and it will all be one horrible mess because I am dreadful and no-one will ever love me properly. Not even Yann, my glorious gigolo. Oh, how I will wish he did! But he will be European and blond and lithe and golden. He will speak several languages well and be the son of an ambassador who has fallen on hard times. I will hate myself for exploiting him, and he will hate himself for being reduced to women such as me. He'll only visit me once in prison and everyone will assume he is my son and it will be awkward.

So you see how I would be in need of romantic advice, like.

Her fontanelle is so soft. I can't stop stroking it, and I'm really worried I will be too rough and put my finger through her brain or something. Velvet-soft she is, my little girl. Velvet soft and full of screams. She wants it all, all the milk, all the comfort, all of it. And I want her to have it.

Dad tried to have another talk with me last night before Robb came over. It was about boys but ended up being about something else as well.

'This Robb with two bees fella.'

'Yes?'

'Are you seeing him?'

'I'm not sure.' We were both staring at the wallpaper. Dad's hands were on his knees.

'Well, if you ever want to go to a lady-doctor and get yourself sorted out, I can arrange that.'

'Get myself sorted out?'

Quote from Prim's mum's diary

'Not that I'm encouraging that sort of behaviour. But if it is a thing that's going to happen, I'd rather you were taking care of yourself. Your sexual health.'

'MY WHAT?' I asked.

'Don't make me repeat it, Prim.'

'I won't, Fintan.'

'And you're my little girl, so it's hard for me to think of you as a sexual being, but if you ever need any advice or anything ...'

'What, like sex-tips?'

'No. NO. Like sexual health advice. Jesus.' He looked supremely flustered.

I was glad. I'd said that sex-tips thing to try and dock the conversation where it was.

'Anyway, I know there's pressure on teen girls to be sexual these days.'

'Dad ...'

'Let me finish.'

'Dad.' I put my hand on his arm.

'What?'

'You do NOT need to be having this conversation with me. The Internet is a valuable tool and I already know a lot about my – sexual health.'

His face looked as down-trodden and disgusted as mine felt.

'The Internet is no substitute for a parent. And it's very easy to make a mistake, Prim. One slip and you're left with the consequences for years to come.'

'Like you were with me?' I asked him. He shook his head.

'I wouldn't swap you for anything, you know that. And actually, I meant that ...'

'What?'

'Well. It's very easy to get caught up in the heat of the moment and even adults don't always do the right thing, so I feel that it's important that I tell you you're supported. In your choices.'

'MY SEXUAL CHOICES?'

'Yes.'

'What else, Dad?'

I could see something fluttering in his throat, waiting to get out. When you know a person well, you get a kind of handle on their tics that makes it way harder for them to lie to you.

'Well.'

'It is not going to be any weirder a conversation than the one we just had. And once it's out there, we can forget it.'

'Well ...'

'Out with it, or I'll just assume it's cancer and act accordingly.'

'Sorrel. We ...'

'You've broken up?'

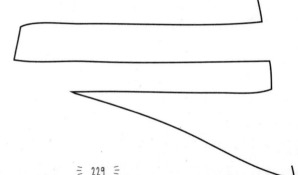

Deirdre Sullivan

'We're
going
to have
a baby.'

And what do you say to a thing like that

Loads of things, but Robb with two bees rang the doorbell and my head was melting but I had to entertain him and hang out watching movies and holding Dad's news inside me like it was a bomb that would go off once its name was spoken out loud.

At first, Fintan made himself thoroughly scarce as soon as Robb was around, which is uncharacteristic of him, because normally he's all 'A boy, eh?' and peering around corners curiously and leaving doors open and things. And that is just with Joel. I don't know if I've had a boy who wasn't Joel over here before. Syzmon and Caleb when we were watching movies in a big group but not otherwise.

I took Robb up to my room and sat on my bed and asked him questions about boarding school while he alphabetised my books and CDs. I don't have a lot of CDs. The ones I have mainly used to belong to Mum. And the things I have belonging to her are kind of precious, because Dad threw out a lot of her stuff quite soon after she died. Like, bundled up in bin bags and into the charity shop. This is another example of thoughtlessness on his part.

Not that I am stuck for such examples. I can't believe he knocked Sorrel up. How far along is she? I wonder.

Because normally you wait three months before you tell people, but I don't think that rule counts for family. And if she's told him, I assume she wants to keep it. I mean, she isn't coming to London with us or anything. So there's that.

I wonder if it's Dad's.

It has to be. I mean, she's very honest. I know she has a lot of boyfriends and things, but I don't think I remember her ever having more than one at the same time. If they were exclusive, which I don't know if she and Dad even are.

'This is a really good album!' exclaimed Robb, brandishing one of Mum's more angry music choices.

'Yeah, I like it too. It used to be my mum's.'

'Cool. My mum likes crooners.' He said this in the same tone of voice as Anne will say 'Duncan' when she finds out about him.

'Crooners?' I was aghast. 'Like old guys in colouredy tuxedos singing the kind of songs you hear in lifts?'

'Not just old guys. Young men do it too.' He sounded despondent.

'Ugh.'

'I know. We go to France every summer and I have to listen to their music choices the whole time. I'm not allowed to play my music until I have a driver's licence.'

'Does your *dad* have good taste in music?' I asked.

'He likes rural comedy songs.'

EEP.

'Jesus.'

'I'd rather listen to the Leaving Cert aural back catalogue.'

'Me too, I think. Fintan has pretty good taste in music. Sadly, he has many other qualities as well.'

'Sadly?'

'Well, he's a dad. He wears socks under his sandals.'

'My dad too. Sometimes he pulls them up, so there's only, like, a foot of skin visible between where his socks end and his shorts begin.'

I could easily have out-dadded him by saying that Dad was after impregnating my late mum's best friend, but I don't know Robb with two bees well enough to share that, so I asked about his holidays instead.

'Are you going to France this summer?'

'The last two weeks of August. We're going to Dijon.'

'With the mustard?' I'm not gone on mustard but I know a bit about it because Dad lathers it on to things with gusto.

'Yeah. It's going to be *amazing*.' He italicised amazing with his voice. It was impressive.

'I bet.'

'And then they pack me off to school again, until October.'

'You like it, though.'

'Yeah. I like it.'

He didn't sound too happy as he said it, though. I kind of wanted to hug him or something, but I didn't. He crawled up to the bed, and started looking through the pile of books beside it. I normally only read one book at a time, but I'm reading three at the moment, because one is short stories, so you can read it as a snack. Then there's the book of Tennessee Williams plays because they are summery and pretty and sad and then there is the book about sexy earls. Robb chose to pick on the sexy earl book.

Because
OF COURSE
he did.

'You read this trash?' he asked.

'Yeah.'

'I thought you were supposed to be clever.'

'Do you know what an entailment is?' I asked.

'No.'

'Can you explain to me the ins and outs of Regency-era British family law?'

'No.'

'Then maybe YOU should read *Earl Interrupted*.'

'Hmmm.'

He opened a page. It was, as I had kind of known it was going to be, full of sex. I blushed a little. So did he.

'Prim. This is ...' His voice went low, in case anyone would hear us. 'This is *lady-porn*.'

'Not all of it. And I prefer the term Regency romance.' I folded my hands into my lap and sat straight-backed, like a decent governess.

'Are ALL girl-books like this?'

'I resent the term "girl-books". Books don't have genitals.'

'This one does.'

'Only from chapter twenty-three on, and it's both kinds so that hardly genders it.'

'You know what I mean, romance novels or whatever. Are they all this ... explicit?'

'That's not the worst of them. It's like, only ten per cent sex. Most of it is build-up.'

'Oh.'

'Oh, what?'

Robb looked as though he were about to cry. His lower lip trembled and his eyebrows did a thing like they were deciding to be sad but then decided to be angry and then went back to normal all in the space of five seconds.

'My nana reads these. Like, all the time. She gets them out of the library.'

'Why shouldn't she? Besides, it's like the most socially acceptable form of porn there is. There aren't any pictures. Apart from mind-pictures. And people have those sometimes, even without books featuring the adventures of a sexy yet relatable earl and his sensitive yet damaged soul-mate the hot governess.'

I was actually properly embarrassed and I wanted to stop talking but I couldn't. It was like Steve the goblin with the drinking. I knew that the words should stop coming out. The words like 'genitals' and 'sex' and '*explicit*' and, oh God, '*mind-pictures*'. I should not have let him open the book and encouraged the conversation about it. It made everything pure tense, because the thought of earl sex was there in the room, glowering at us. Sexily.

Robb coughed.

I blinked.

'This is almost as awkward as that time I told you that thing about the ducks, isn't it?'

'Yes. YES! Why did you tell me that?'

'I don't know. If I knew why I do the things I do, I would just stop it and not do them. I wish it were that simple.' He was playing with the catches on the bottom of my quilt and not looking at me.

'That would be good for me as well, I think.' I was staring at his hands but I could feel his eyes on my neck.

And then we started kissing. Kissing is a really nice way to spend, like, forty-five to fifty minutes. At first, when Robb kissed me, I really noticed his teeth, and I still did, but with a bit of practice we seemed to come together in a softer, nicer way. He did this weird thing though. He, like, put his tongue in my ear. *And I kind of liked it.* Does this make me a terrible lady-pervert, well suited to my reading material?

I mean, I know ear-shifting is hardly a sex act. But it was so unexpected. I was, like, 'This is going to be pure weird,' and, '*Oh.*' I have never, ever discussed ear-shifting with anyone. I must ask Ciara about it. She's gotten up

to some devilment in her time and will surely weigh in on the subject in a clear-eyed and non-judgemental manner.

I was very glad I'd cleaned my ears that morning. He gave them quite an attentive seeing-to.

After a bit of kissing, though, I kind of started thinking about Dad and Sorrel and so I had to call a halt. Because they have no place in that section of my brain.

'Do you want a cup of tea or something?' I asked.

'OK.'

Robb with two bees is quite a biddable young gent, for all that he disapproves of my reading choices and didn't know where Bolivia was. As we drank the tea, he tried to hold my hand.

'I need that to dunk my biscuits, Robb.'

'Right. Sorry.'

'It's OK. You can hold my hand afterwards.'

I smiled at him. He smiled back.

Fintan came in and we both stopped smiling. Me because I was reminded of his fertility and poor judgement and Robb because Dad was glaring at him in a threatening manner. The kind of manner that says, 'When I begin to talk, I am going to address you as "young man". But what I'll actually mean is "loathsome boy".'

'Hello, Rob-buh'

'It's just Robb,' I said.

'Oh, I thought that you had two bees.'

'FINTAN!'

'My name is Dad, Primrose.'

'I do, but it's pronounced the same.' Robb looked at Fintan the way a hedgehog looks at a busy road it is doomed to cross.

'So ... what film are we watching?' Fintan asked, clearly intent on ruining my life.

He looked Robb up and down and clearly decided that this young man was a threat of some kind. He put the kettle on again and smiled. I looked at Robb. He looked at me.

Oh God.

'We hadn't decided yet. Probably something set in a high school?' I said. Dad hated high-school movies. He said they were too high-pitched.

'Wonderful. I'll watch too. It will afford me some insight into the teenage mind.'

He slapped his hands down on his jeans and brushed off imaginary dirt as though it was made of Robb. DE.LIB.ER.ATE.LY.

'What kind of film do you want to watch, Mr Leary?' said Robb.

Oh God.

'My name,' said Dad, 'is Fintan Hamilton.' And written between the lines of dialogue was this: *and you would do well to remember it, lest I garrotte you.*

Whereupon Robb actually asked my dad's permission to go to the bathroom. Fintan wrinkled his brow.

'Number One or Number Two?'

'*What?*'

'I'm only messing, lad, off you trot.' He smiled.

It reminded me of the way that a dog will roll over and show its throat to another dog to show submission. Robb had recognised who the alpha male in the house was. Which you'd think would have made it increasingly difficult for me to fancy him, but you'd be wrong. Seeing my kissing companion reduced to requesting bathroom breaks so he could get away from my dad awoke something protective in me.

Once Robb had closed the door, I properly hissed at dad.

'FINTAN!'

'My name is Dad. I told you.'

'Dads are nice. And you, Fintan, are being mean.'

Dad looked at me, all innocence.

'I don't know what you're talking about.'

'You totally do. Come on.'

He had the grace to look a little bashful.

'I just wanted to get the measure of him, Primmy.'

'You do not get the measure of someone by cutting them down to size and then measuring them. You broke my sort-of-boyfriend, Fintan.'

'What's a sort-of-boyfriend? Is it one of those *friends with benefits* things I read about online?'

I started to really notice the veins on his forehead. They were kind of *purpling* with emotion, if that can be a verb.

'No. **NO**. I just haven't decided if I like him enough to be, like, *exclusive*.'

Something like horror passed over my father's face. I think that I had properly scandalised him.

Robb came back in. He looked a bit wan. 'I was thinking we could watch that Stones documentary I brought on my memory stick.'

Fintan looked at him. 'The Scorsese one?'

Scorsese is a director old dudes and young dudes who think old dudes are cool and want to emulate them like.

'Yeah.'

'You might not be a total loss, my boy,' said Fintan, who is vastly under-qualified to make such judgements.

Robb, who had apparently forgotten the list of creepy facts about Fintan I had shared with him not an hour beforehand, looked as though he had been given a birthday present made of winning lottery tickets.

'Thank you, Mr Hamilton.'

Dad nodded approvingly. He patted him on the shoulder. I got a little squirmy. Was Robb, like, *flirting* with my dad? Something was definitely going on with the two of them. They thoroughly enjoyed the film. I crocheted a little and they mocked me for being a granny. I don't even know what I'm making, actually. It started off round, but it's more of a square shape at the moment. I think it might ultimately end up a blanket.

Robb's mum came to pick him up around half ten. He shook Fintan's hand, and went to give me a hug, but looked at Dad and shook mine too. I thought of his hands

SOCKS AND SANDALS.

on my tummy on the bed earlier that evening. Such different touches.

His mum's car drove away and it was me, Dad and my outrage.

'You did

NOT

just call him

"MY BOY"

like an aging paedophile, Fintan.'

'What? No. You can't talk to me like that. Go to your room.'

He was properly bristling at me. Sometimes he gets funny when I'm cheeky. All outraged and junk. It's like he's forgotten my actual personality.

'I won't,' I said, reminding him of my actual personality. And outrage. He demurred, like a lady in one of my novels.

'I meant for it to be paternal. He was only gagging for a bit of approval.'

'Robb is not *gagging* for anything that you can give him.'

'And he won't gag for anything you can give him either by the time I'm finished with him.'

'You're not allowed to bully him, Dad. That's not OK.'

'Of course it is OK. I am your father.'

'I know you are, Mr Leary.'

He did the kind of laugh that is also a grunt. 'Jesus, he got my back right up there.'

'Why?'

'I just don't like being reminded of your mum when I'm in the middle of parenting.'

'That was parenting?'

'Yes.'

'Why don't you like being reminded of Mum?' I interlaced my fingers and leaned back in my chair, like a total Caroline.

'I don't mind it. I think about your mother all the time. But when I'm in the middle of trying to be a dad, it kind of irks me. Like she's watching me and doing that clucking thing she used to do when I swept the floor wrong.'

I did the clucking thing. He laughed.

'That's the one. I just. I want to do this right. I want you to have everything. But I can't be a mother. And I'm still kind of getting father lessons.'

'You're doing OK, Fintan. It's been three and a bit years. You've got the hang.'

'I thought I had. But then I knocked up Sorrel, and you got boyfriends.'

'How long had you been seeing Sorrel before you asked me if it was OK to ask her on a date?'

'We weren't seeing each other, not exactly. She was giving me Indian head massages and things were happening. And we had a talk and I wanted to get your OK before we made it serious, but it was kind of too late by then because I'm going to be a father again.'

'Don't ask her to marry you. Until the baby is, like, one. Or three. Three seems a good number.'

'I won't. It won't be like it was when Bláth had you. I know you don't think it, but thirty-four is young. Or it was for me. I didn't feel like a grown-up, but I got myself into a grown-up situation and felt the need to act accordingly. To do the right thing, you know.'

'The right thing is only the right thing if it is actually the right thing, Dad.'

'You are confusing and wise. Where did I get you at all?'

'From a toxic relationship with an eighteen-year-old college student.'

'Ah, yeah. That'd do it.'

'And please don't say "knocked-up", Dad. It kind of belittles it. I mean, I'm going to have a brother or sister.'

'I just. I hate saying "impregnated". And "got Sorrel pregnant" is so removed. It's not a thing she'll have to deal with on her own. I'm going to be there.'

'And you really don't want to go down the "we're pregnant" road like Uncle Patsy,' I said.

'That's a dark road. It's not a road for a man to go down lightly.'

'I read in this historical romance novel once –'

'Those things.'

'Yeah,' I said. 'Those things. Anyway, back in the day, they used to say a woman was "with squirrel". That seemed kind of cute to me.'

'I quite like that. And Sorrel might as well ...'

'So no more knocking-up talk.'

'Fine. Sorrel is with squirrel. We're very happy. I hope that you are too. About the squirrel.'

'I'm on the fence. Are we still going to London?'

'Of course. I should take you on more holidays, really. I work all the time and I know it isn't fair on you.'

'It's fine. Can we go to the British Museum?'

'Yes.'

'And lament our nation's plundered treasures?'

'Ireland doesn't actually have all that many plundered treasures in there, Prim.'

'We could pretend to be Greek!'

'Will it involve silly accents and false beards?'

'No.' (Yes.)

'Grand so.'

We finished our tea. The last cup I had from the pot was almost cold. I love my dad. He is the worst but also occasionally the best. I wonder if I could give him side-burns. Greek men could totally have side-burns. They're allowed to have whatever they want. Except for most of the Parthenon. I couldn't say to Robb about the baby. I thought about it, in my room, but didn't. I didn't want my mouth to form the words and make it real. Once it's out there, known about, I'll have to decide what I think about it. And I don't know. And Robb would have made a snarky comment maybe, or an awkward joke. And things were nice. I didn't want to ruin it.

How do I feel about you, Robb? I wish I fully knew. His fingers brushed the small bumps of my scars so tenderly. He didn't say a thing. I wonder if we'll ever be close enough for him to ask me what they are. For me to tell him. Probably not. He's going off to France and then to school. I think that it would take months and maybe years to get that close to someone. That's the thing about physical stuff, it rushes friendships. And you think, *He's touched my boobs, I should be able to tell him about cutting.*

That was a mistake I kind of made with Kevin early on. I thought that if I gave him enough of me, then he would be my boyfriend. That we would be closer and closer and closer until we were a unit. It doesn't work that way. He'd listen and then kiss me and I thought that maybe if I took it a little further this time then we would be closer. Not that I didn't want to. Because I did. I just wanted the emotional stuff as well. And I thought the one would lead to the other. Because it did for me. I kind of liked him and then he made me feel a thousand ways and then I REALLY liked him. Caps lock really. That much. I don't know. I'm probably going to make the same mistakes with Robb. He probably won't want me once he has me. Because he doesn't really have me yet. I'm holding on to distance. Because the closer I get to him, the more rope I fear he'll give me.

A little flower. That's what she reminds me of. I can't call her Cowslip, though. I'd only get away with that till school starts and that's, what, four years?

That's only five per cent of a person's life.

People live longer now.

Felix got his Leaving Cert results today. He got 450 points. I texted him to wish him luck and things. It's a big deal. He's kind of annoyed, because he was hoping to get the points for sound engineering as opposed to science, but it looks like he's going to have to fight with Mary about it a bit. I hope he gets to follow his dream. I feel like boy-crushes should be allowed to fly free, to be awesome where they wilt. But that's a girl thing as opposed to a mum thing. Mums tend to want what's best for you. Only they sometimes get what's best for you mixed up with what they would do in your shoes or what a layman would do. Which clouds things a little.

'I want Felix to be happy,' said Ella, who was eating a cheese fry. A whole bowl of them, as a matter of fact. Not just like one HUGE one on a plate. One time, me and Ciara went to this diner near Stephen's Green and

Quote from Prim's mum's diary

we got a large chips to share, and there was like one big chip in the middle of the bowl which was like seven improperly separated chips. It was amazing. We will always remember it.

'Remember the big chip, Prim?' asked Ciara, who is a superlative human being.

'I do. Do you still have the picture on your phone?'

'Of course.'

We looked at The Big Chip, and Ella rolled her eyes to heaven. She was not around for the advent of The Big Chip and I don't think she gets quite how magnificent it was.

'I can't believe you're going to London, like, *tomorrow*.' Ciara was disgusted. 'It's going to be so dear to text you.'

'You could always just not text me.'

'What, for a whole week? Yeah, right.'

Ella was still munching the cheese fry. She chews her food very methodically.

'It's weird, isn't it,' she said, 'how we always have to text each other about things? Like, if we don't, maybe they didn't really happen?'

I said 'Yes' and Ciara said 'No' at the exact same time and then we all looked at each other and laughed a bit.

But it *is* weird, how we tell each other everything. And non-disclosure can be perceived as a sort of insult, like, *You don't trust me enough to tell me this and why.* There are things I don't want to tell people, things I don't want to talk about and don't. But they are a part of me, like my eyes and face and undying love for Ella's older brother. And it doesn't mean anything when I don't share them with Ciara or Ella. It's not spiteful or whatever. But then, when you do tell people stuff, they know more bits of you and little by little you become closer. It's not that I want to distance myself from Ciara or Ella or Joel when I don't talk about the sad bits. It's just I want to distance *myself* from things that make me sad. Deliberately pushing them away and focusing on all that's wonderful, like kissing clever boys and admiring The Big Chip. I loved that chip.

Ella hasn't changed her mind about Caleb. They haven't met up since the party, but they are going to and there will be some kissing when they do. They talk online a lot.

Ciara misses Syzmon. He hasn't been texting her as much and has been posting pictures of himself hanging out with friends who are not her, drinking things and smiling. She knows it isn't fair to want him to be sadder than he is.

'No-one posts pictures of themselves weeping and listening to power ballads on the Internet, Ciara. No-one we know anyway. The Internet is for your best self. You know Syzmon's in bits.'

'Tell me again about how sad he was at the party.'

'SooOO sad,' said Ella, using lots of vowels to emphasise the woe.

'Properly destroyed,' I added. 'I thought he was going to cry at one point.'

'Thanks, guys, I really needed that.'

We went around the shops for a bit and I bought a sparkly blue mini-skirt because it was four euro. After Ella left, Ciara and I went for tea and cake.

'I feel a bit bad for wanting Syzmon to be upset. It's not that I wish him ill, it's just that I'm upset and he should be that way as well, I think.'

'It's normal. You don't want to be easy to get over.'

'Yeah. I want to be, like, important. One of my favourite things about being with him was how important he made me feel. I mean, he really thought I was amazing.'

'You *are* amazing and it's OK to want him to be sad about it. You were together for ages, like sixteen per cent of your lives or something.'

'Yeah. That is a huge chunk of my life. I only have another eighty-four per cent left.'

'That's not how that sum works, Ciara.'

I unfolded a paper napkin and jotted it down to show her.

'Ugh. That was a stupid mistake. Emotions.' She smiled and did that thing where she adjusts her hair with two hands like she is steering it.

'Emotions cloud things,' I agreed.

'How very Caroline of you,' said Ciara.

'Are you still seeing her?' I asked.

'Yeah, like once every six weeks now. How about you?'

'Dad's making me go weekly for the next while. Because of my raging alcoholism.'

'I talk of little else when I'm in her office,' Ciara said and put her hand on mine. 'I'm glad you're finally getting the help you need.'

Then there was some cackling. I wonder how Caroline will take the pregnancy thing, actually. Maybe I should be having more feelings about it. I kind of feel like I should be angrier, or sadder, or something.

Something negative. I haven't texted Sorrel yet. Maybe when I text Sorrel things will coalesce into something more solid.

I should text Sorrel. I know I should. To congratulate her, I suppose. That would be the traditional approach.

I kind of don't want to, though. But what to say instead? 'I know, and I'm not cross. I won't berate you. Optional ☺'

That definitely wouldn't be good enough.

Fintan is building up to breaking up with me.

I can feel it welling up in him. Like a tick about to burst from too much blood.

I wonder if the baby will be a boy or a girl. I'm used to having a little brother, because of Marcus, so I could help with a boy. I've grown out of putting false moustaches onto babies. I used to think it was the funniest thing ever. But if you do something often enough, it kind of loses its glow. I have adhered moustaches to infants, wobblers and toddlers approximately 216 times since I was eleven years old. Most of them were Marcus. If something is funny 216 times, it is probably a decent joke, even if it doesn't work any more. Maybe I'm maturer? Like a fine cheese.

I wonder if I'll love the baby.

I was right. About Fintan.

She's two days old and I am looking at her and I'm crying and telling her we'll be OK.

In a while, I'll probably believe it.

Our flight is early so Joel is staying over. He's sitting on my bed, and I am on the floor, leaning against it. I never use the rocking chair in my room as, like, a seat. It's weird how things take on roles. I mean, that chair was probably a chair for ages. It's antique. I don't know how antique but it's antique. And now, it sits in my room, a majestic clothes-balancer. I used to pet my Roderick on it sometimes. When I moved here first. I have more clothes now. I think it's because I've been the same size for a while. Dad used to find it really weird how fast I grew, how things would need replacing very soon. There are certain suits and pairs of shoes he's had for decades. Imagine being the same size for a decade! How solid that would feel! How comfortable! My father used to be a weekend dad and then he was a Fintan and now he is a proper all-day dad. I wonder how the new kid will divide him, if he will have less time for me. If he will love me less. I don't think parents work that way, not normally. But there's always a chance that something weird will happen when there are people involved.

Quote from Prim's mum's diary

Sorrel will probably love me less. I texted her.

> I know. I'm happy for you and we'll chat when I
> get back from London. ☺

> Good to know. What do you think of the first
> name Squirrel? Your dad gave me the idea. Chat
> soon x

I think that was OK. Appropriate. Maybe when it is a grey smudge on a photo I will feel like it is real. Maybe when it is a growth under the skin and jutting out through tie-dye or crushed velvet. Maybe when I touch to feel it kick. I've never felt a baby kick before. When I was small, I one time did feel kittens. There was a honey-coloured cat named Farrah in our neighbour's house, she was a stray, they took her in and found out she was pregnant. She was a cat who was shaped like a kitten, all fine angles, delicate. China-dainty. She gave birth to eight little kits. Seven breathing, one dead. We held a funeral for the dead one in my back garden. I think that was the first funeral I ever went to. Mum held my hand and we sang the cat a song I'd learnt at play-group. She was sitting in a box the neighbour kids had brought into the garden. Still and regal, like a duchess, she washed herself while all the humans grieved.

The week before the cat had had her babies, I was over at the house. Mum was at work and I was being minded. Eric, who was seven and older than me, put my fat hand onto Farrah's stomach and said, 'Feel.'

I did, and there were, like, loads of legs. Did I detect an ear? It was a miracle. All those angles bruising through the soft.

After the kitten died, the grass was wet and Mum had handcream on her hands and they were greasy. I said 'I'm sorry, Farrah,' and I shook her paw, just like it was a hand. Eric told me that's what's done at funerals. Seven years and he was shaking mine. So many people came out of the woodwork when Mum died and then faded right back in as quick as anything. Like when you see a picture in a cloud and when you look back up it's something else, a thing that's unfamiliar.

If something can die does that make it alive? Six weeks pregnant, that's all Sorrel is. It's just begun. Now is the dangerous time. You don't say the words out loud until you're fairly sure what's growing in you won't die. They must have done it right before my English paper one. Made the baby. What will it think of me, I wonder? If I move out for college when it's two, will it still be my family? Will it even live with me and Fintan? Is Sorrel moving in now? I can't think. There are a lot of things to be resolved. But in another six weeks, the baby will be a fixed point. Real and spoken of and coming. It will not be a secret any more. It's hard to keep a person secret. Even when we're little we're too big.

'Babies are catalysts – you react to them and change your life. Primrose Ivy Leary will not have her feeds delayed, heartbreak or no. I left the hospital today. I packed my engagement ring in with the bottles. I think I'm going to throw it in the Liffey.

Joel helped me pack. I showed him my blue mini-skirt and he hated it, but I'm going to bring it anyway. I have an outfit planned. It's hard enough to sort out seven pairs of matching socks. I had to upend my drawer.

'So … you and Duncan?'

'What about us?' He was keeping his face neutral.

'Oh, come on. Stop trying to be mature. You're dying to tell me.'

'Well, Prim.' His face did that thing where his mouth gets betrayed by his eyebrows. 'If you must know, we've been kind of … building up.'

'To things?'

'Obviously.' Eyebrows and mouth were on the same page now. Lofty.

Quote from Prim's mum's diary

'Well, you obviously wanted to tell me about things when you sent that text.'

'Yeah, well. To be honest it felt kind of like ...'

'Like?'

'A thing that I should inform you about as opposed to something I actually wanted to talk about. I mean, I have no idea how to talk about, like, *sex*. How much can you say before you're saying too much? I don't want to hurt Duncan or anything. He's too important. Prim, I think I *love* him.'

Oh dear. What do you say to that? I was trying really hard to set my facial features to 'supportive' and 'under-standing' but it was hard. My eyebrows had certain things they needed to communicate via muscular contractions and suchlike.

'I'm pleased for you. I'd like to fall in love.'

'I don't know if you would.'

'I think I would.'

'But, like, it's really hard.' His face dispersed into pale and blotchy sections. 'I don't want to say it first. I know he likes me, but I have all these feelings and they well up in me and I'm worried they'll spill out.'

'And what? You'll tell him?'

'I can't say "I love you" first. He'll think I'm childish.'

'Not if he says it back.'

'I don't think that he will, though.'

I wanted to argue but his face was set and I didn't want to shake it in case it cracked again. I hate it when Joel cries. It's like my heart starts crying too beside him.

'And have you ...?'

'We've been working up to it. These things take time.'

'I know.'

'So – I feel like I have probably lost a portion of my virginity. Like, two-thirds of it.'

I was impressed. 'That's a fair whack of virginity.'

'I know.'

We paused for a moment to mull.

'Ciara said to me one time that when you are in love, there are loads of little first times. I don't think she fully meant sex things though.'

'It's hard to imagine Ciara doing sex things. She's very prim,' said Joel, as though it were somehow massively easy to imagine our other friends doing sex things. The creep.

'Ciara can be messy. Just because her nails are perfect doesn't mean her head is.'

'Fair enough.' He shrugged.

'Two-thirds, eh? I like your theory. I wonder if Kevin took a bit of my virginity? Not, like, much. Maybe five per cent or something. That time in the wardrobe.'

'Nope. With straight people it has to be the full thing or it doesn't count.'

'That is not very open-minded of you. I think it's probably something everyone defines for themselves. When it feels right ...'

At this point Joel said, 'Hmmm,' and looked off into the distance. I love when he does this because it makes me feel very wise indeed. I hope Duncan loves him back. He deserves to be loved. Even if it is by a problematic older gent with a tattoo of a pigeon on his calf. Joel showed me a picture of it on his phone. It's not very nice. The pigeon looks a bit baleful, to be honest. I'd like to get a tattoo when I'm older. A cowslip on my ribcage, near my heart.

Plant-based names are really appealing to me. Fintan told me I was not to call her Cowslip. As if he had any right to tell me what to do any more.

e got up early. Dad was stoic on the drive to the airport. He gave me the passports and print-outs. I was in charge of them, apparently.

'Why me? You are the grown-up.'

He looked a bit abashed. 'Well, it'll be up to you because I'll be taking this.' He produced a chalky little pill from his pocket. 'An hour or so prior to flight.'

'So soon.'

'Yes. And I won't be good for much after that.'

'What's the pill for, Fintan?' Joel was curious. His OLD MAN boyfriend had probably familiarised him with illegal pills of all kinds as well as made him feel insufficiently loved.

'Well, Joel. Some people don't enjoy air travel. And this pill helps them to journey more smoothly.'

Quote from Prim's mum's diary

'It's a one-hour flight, Fintan. Can't you suck it up?' I asked him, not unkindly. OK, pretty unkindly.

'No. I would have already sucked it up if I was able to suck it up.'

'Be nice to him, Primrose. It's probably, like, a phobia or something.' I think Joel basically just wanted my dad to stop saying the word *suck* and take us on our holidays.

'Thanks, Joel,' said Fintan. 'I'm not sure what it is that frightens me. It's a combination of being in an enclosed space and being really high up.'

'Yes. It is called a plane, Dad. People go on them every day. Sometimes for, like, eighteen or nineteen hours.'

'I have gone on long-haul flights, Prim. I don't let it stop me. I just take these and then I feel calm and dozy. But I occasionally misplace things, so I'm giving you my passport.'

'What do you do when you're travelling by yourself?' I asked.

'I wait till I've checked in. If it's long-haul, it usually has worn off by the time we're landing. Don't look at me like that. I'm not going to be *zonked* or anything. Not like you were at that party.'

'He has you there, Prim.'

Joel gets on great with my dad since he bought him crepes for being gay. They got on OK before, but now they, like, *side* with each other. It is sickening.

'He does **NOT** have me. I am tolerant and helpful,' I said, putting the passports in my handbag and resolving to hold his to ransom once we got to London. I quite fancied some theatre tickets. Something with plaintive singing and emboldened hearts in. I wasn't picky.

I really like airports. I assumed Dad would too, because he has to travel for work so much. But no. He glared at the building, as though it were somehow its fault that he was going to have to go up in the sky and be frightened.

'Can I get a travel hair-straightener?' I asked.

'Don't be asking me for things, Prim. Particularly after I've taken the pill.'

'Will you be, like, suggestible and stuff?' I wondered.

'I'm not sure.'

He was sure. I could tell by the face on him. He just didn't want to say.

'We won't take advantage of you, Fintan,' Joel promised.

'I might,' I said.

'I'll make sure she doesn't.'

'Thank you, Joel.'

THINGS I KNOW
THAT FINTAN DOESN'T

1.

Joel is not always to be trusted.

2.

He really wants a new MP3 player.

3.

There's always the way back.

😐

From what I have heard about tranquillisers I was expecting him to be zonked out of it, but he was pretty lucid. I've seen him worse. Like, when he's woken up unexpectedly from a sofa-nap. Or surprised by a high-pitched noise. The discombobulation level was medium at most.

In the airport, we had tea and a little chocolate and Dad took out his book and pretended to read it while myself and Joel chatted. He was not fooling anyone, getting through, like, half a page and following our conversation like it was an audio-book he occasionally had opinions about. He threw in his two cents' worth every now and then.

'That one.' (When Karen was mentioned.)

'You're only young once.' (When Joel was debating a septum piercing.)

'Not under my roof, you won't.' (When I mentioned the possibility of a tattoo.)

It was really – 'companionable' is the word I'm looking for, I suppose. I haven't used that word in ages, in my head or written down. A safe, cosy kind of lull between bits of life is what we had curling up on seats that all faced the same way at our gate until the flight was boarding and we switched off our phones. Well, Joel and I did. Dad left his till the last minute. Just in case anyone wanted to talk to a slightly bewildered businessman. I wonder is flight-medication conference-calling more or less socially acceptable than drunk-dialling? Or is it worse? It's probably worse. I bet Dad's drunk dialled Hedda a couple of times. Mum drunk dialled him. I rarely get drunk enough to drunk-dial Kevin, preferring to embarrass myself in front of him in other, sober ways.

It's kind of acceptable to humiliate yourself in front of an ex. Not enjoyable. But we have all been there, texting our different-shaped Kevins at three o' clock in the morning with courage in our hearts and feelings running through our veins making everything an emotional imperative. I'd probably text Robb instead of Kevin late at night-time now. He'd probably text back as well. I wonder why he likes me. Joel thinks it's because I'm beautiful. He told me that when Dad went to the bathroom.

'I'm not. Size of me. Face on me. Personality on me.'

'You are medium-sized and you go in and out in the right places. Your face is my favourite face – you're always one step away from plotting something. And your personality belongs to my best friend. So clearly Robb is a discerning individual.'

'Ugh.'

Dad came back from the bathroom and joined us.

'I don't know why everyone gets up to queue,' he said. 'The seats are assigned.'

'Programming?'

Dad agreed. 'You're right. Let's sit back down.'

'I don't want to lose my meaningless place in the queue, though.' Joel pretend sulked. In fairness to him, there were about twenty people behind us. And it felt a bit like we were winning the game. The boring, pointless game.

So we stayed and handed in our boarding passes and got them scanned and took our seats. Dad was looking a little bit drained about the face. He took the aisle so he wouldn't see out the window. I was in the middle, gazing over Joel at the tarmac of the runway and the green of the grass beyond it. There's something really magic about planes: you're on the ground and then, little by little, layer by layer, the plane balances up. Tens of thousands of feet above the ground and you can see the tops of things you've only ever seen the bottom of, like clouds and cities. Dad was breathing deep.

Joel looked at him. 'Prim doesn't think she's beautiful.'

Dad looked at me. 'Don't be ridiculous. She's stunning. Best thing I've ever done.'

'Shut up, Dad,' I said but I was smiling.

The plane was mounting sky. My father gulped. I took his hand. The skin on it was dry and slightly, oh-so-slightly wrinkled. He squeezed and I squeezed back and smiled at him. Joel took my other hand in his. I felt a callous in his index finger brush against my thumb. And something else, which probably was love.

And up we flew.

I look at Fintan and I think we probably won't last but now, right now, I'm happy. 'She's 0,' I say to him, '0 years old. Isn't that amazing?' and his face lights up and he says yes it is, and reaches his arms out to hold her and it hurts to take her skin from mine. We couldn't have done that yesterday, I think. Yesterday you were a bit of me and now you're you. I've never had an always love so quick as this, and maybe not at all before. It's strange and new and fathomless. I want to help her navigate the world so carefully. My little smudge who turned into a bump who turned into a person.

Her chubby little hand around his thumb and he is smiling. We are a family, together in this moment.

Bláthnaid.
Primrose.
Fintan.   .... Quote from Prim's mum's diary

APPENDIX

1.

A body-part that may have been to let us digest grass once upon a time. It goes on your large intestine and sometimes gets inflamed.

2.

An extra section at the end of the book, featuring additional matter.

3.

A thing this book will have.

Ciara's checklist
of wants in a Boyfriend

1. Is hot.
2. Enjoys watching ~~High School Musical~~ the films I love.
3. Is kind.
4. Has not ever been a bully.
5. Likes children.
6. Is not afraid of commitment.
7. Dresses well.
8. Has nice hair. Mid-length, no buzz cuts, skin-heads or people with long luxurious metaller heads on them. Or mullets.
9. Is not gay.
10. Does not fancy anyone except me.
11. Gives me presents on Valentine's Day.
12. Gives me presents on my birthday.
13. Gives me presents on our anniversaries.
14. Gives me presents on our monthaversaries.
15. Gives me presents just because.
16. Pays for my food and cinema tickets when we go out together.
17. Is not materialistic.
18. Is good at sports.
19. Isn't OBSESSED with sports.
20. Is confident.

21. But not too confident, not like up-himself or anything.

22. Is kind to children.

23. Is kind to old ladies.

24. Is kind to animals.

25. Offers his seat on the bus to old ladies and pregnant women.

26. Will let me read his text messages - not that I would.

27. Has easily guessable Internet passwords.

28. Is clever.

29. But not too clever.

30. Is socially adept.

31. But not smooth.

32. Is fanciable.

33. But doesn't have loads of girls that fancy him and want to destroy our relationship and take my place. Why must we women be so competitive with each other? It is a tragedy.

34. Has brown eyes.

35. Is not thinner than me.

36. Is taller than me.

37. Can lift me up and carry me if I get to tired to walk.

38. Does not patronise me.

39. Understands me.

40. Will be polite to my mother.

41. Will bring her gifts if he ever gets invited to my house for dinner.

42. Will operate under the unspoken assumption that my mother is a wagon and that I am in the right whenever we argue.

43. ~~Will be nice to Grandma Lily.~~ Would have been nice to Grandma Lily. Will listen to me talk about her and visit her grave with me.

44. Will get on with Prim and Ella and Joel.

45. Will not fancy Prim.

46. Will not fancy Ella.

47. Will not fancy Joel and therefore become ineligible for boyfriendhood. (See point 9.)

48. Will allow me to choose his outfits, within reason. (Not every day, but certainly for special occasions.)

49. Will have cute friends.

50. Will support my philanthropy. (Reading to the seniors, setting up my single girlfriends, etc.)

51. Will respect me for my intellect.

52. Will enjoy the aesthetics of a well-made hat.

53. Will not be bisexual.

54. Will take care of his skin and hair.

55. Will have short, regularly trimmed finger- and toenails.

56. Will not have back-hair.

57. Will not have chest-hair to excess, although a small amount is not only acceptable but encouraged.

58. Will ask my father for permission to marry me, when the time comes.

59. Will get on well, but not too well, with my father.

60. Will not be after me for my money.

61. Will not make fun of me.

62. Will have two distinct eyebrows that do not meet in the middle.

63. Will tweeze in order to comply with point 62, if needs be.

64. Will not tell people that he tweezes his eyebrows.

65. Will wear an aftershave I like.

66. But not to excess.
67. Will let me choose the film in the cinema even if it isn't something he wants to see.
68. Will not be a push-over.
69. Is not overly religious.
70. Is a gentleman.
71. Opens doors for me and guides me through them with his hand on the small of my back.
72. Likes to talk about computer games, especially *Fable*. Not all the time, though.
73. Doesn't mind me being better at computer games than he is because I probably am.
74. Doesn't mind me being better at sewing and hat-making than he is because I definitely am.
75. Cares about the environment: puts things in the right bins.
76. Doesn't drink or take drugs to excess.
77. Drinks a bit, though.
78. Won't judge me if I have a few on a night out.
79. Isn't judgemental about how squeaky I get when I'm around Prim.
80. Isn't judgemental about how quiet I can be sometimes.
81. Doesn't mind that I used to eat my own hair.
82. Will never cheat on me.
83. Constantly tells me I am pretty.
84. Does not comment about how pretty other girls are around me, unless explicitly instructed to do so by me, to boost the self-esteem of a single friend.
85. Understands that I am under a lot of pressure.
86. Is not too demanding.

87. Is a great kisser.
88. Is good at the other physical stuff, with a view to being great at it after a reasonable amount of practice.
89. Does not pressure me to have sex with him.
90. Really, really wants to have sex with me.
91. Does not use crude words to refer to parts of either of our bodies.
92. Does not use crude words to refer to sex and sex-related activities.
93. Enjoys the sunshine.
94. Knows how to mow a lawn.
95. Will mow the lawn for my parents on occasion.
96. Replies to my texts.
97. Will always reply to my texts within an hour, if they contain a question.
98. Always returns my phone calls.
99. Texts and calls me frequently.
100. Is prepared to be 'in a relationship' with me on every social networking site he is on.
101. Does not have hairy fingers, like Syzmon's Uncle Luka.
102. Will give me his jacket if I am cold, even if I have a jacket on already.
103. Will not complain about giving me piggy-backs on nights out where I choose to wear impossibly high heels.
104. Will have a strong and load-bearing spine.
105. Will not hate rats.
106. Will not hate cats.
107. Will not hate babies.

108. Will understand that, while I love babies, I never want to have any and will one day get sterilised so I can be sure not to have any.

109. Will not mind if I choose to live in separate but adjoining houses instead of in the same one.

110. Will be a good cook.

111. Will enjoy painting walls.

112. Will enjoy cleaning windows.

113. Will enjoy hoovering.

114. Will enjoy ironing.

115. If points 110-114 do not apply to him, he will do such a good job of convincing me that they do that I will never know.

116. Will not be a liar, though.

117. Will never hurt my feelings on purpose.

118. If I break up with him, will take it with good grace and mildly continue fancying me until his dying breath.

119. He will eventually have a good job and be able to support me until my millinery business takes off.

120. If he marries me after my millinery business takes off, he will have no problem signing a pre-nup.

121. He will want to live in a city when we are older.

122. If we adopt a child, he will be OK with me naming it Lily if it is a girl.

123. Will shave regularly.

124. Will have clean fingernails.

125. Will have clear skin that doesn't burn or freckle in the sunshine.

126. Will be supportive.

127. Will know my mobile number off by heart.

128. Will know my birthday and our anniversary and monthaversary dates off by heart.

129. Will have a masculine name, like Syzmon.

130. Will have the broad shoulders of a sexy Viking from Prim's mum's dirty books.

131. Will not have the raping and pillaging nature of a sexy Viking from Prim's mum's dirty books. Especially not the first part.

132. Will not have two first names or a double-barrelled last name.

133. Will be kind to his mother.

134. Will not be more influenced by his mother than he is by me.

135. Will get on well with his father.

136. Will wear ties that match my dresses when we go to formal occasions.

137. Will be instrumental in getting his cute friends to take my single friends to the debs, grads, socials and any other formal event that we attend, thereby increasing the amount of fun we will have at these events.

138. Will come to art galleries with me.

139. Will understand that I cannot do housework or engage in physical activities while my nails are drying.

140. Will understand that I am precious about my now mid-length hair, seeing as how it was short/eaten for so long.

141. Will smell like freshly cut grass sometimes.

142. Will know how I take my tea: no sugar, quite weak, with three small drops of milk.

143. Will know what stuff I do not like to eat: mushrooms, asparagus, raisins. Will make sure that I am never served foods containing the above items in his home.

144. Will not be a bigot.
145. Will not be one of those boys who is not homophobic in theory but acts weird and uncomfortable around Joel.
146. Will not act weird around Ella because she has Asperger's. Is allowed to act weird around her because he is impressed by her cleverness.
147. Will not act weird around Prim because of her mum being dead. Is allowed to act weird around her because he is sometimes intimidated by her.
148. Will support me if I choose to become an emancipated minor because of how weirdly pushy my family are being about Grandma Lily's will.
149. Will support me no matter what.
150. Will not support me if I start eating my own hair again. Will intervene to save me from myself.
151. Will not tell my mother if I start eating my own hair again. Will not allow me to show weakness in front of her.
152. Will not be anyone Prim has a crush on.
153. Will not be anyone Ella has a crush on.
154. Will not be related to Brian McAllister.
155. Will not be related to me, even distantly.
156. Will not be weird about me not taking communion since Grandma Lily died.
157. Will not be weird about me going to mass every Sunday since Grandma Lily died.
158. Will be OK with me posting cute pictures of us together/him on Facebook.
159. Will be proud of me.

160. Will be someone I can be proud of.
161. Will have a strong work ethic.
162. Will also have a strong play ethic.
163. Will travel with me.
164. Will have a moderately sized nose.
165. Will not squeeze his spots or pick his ears in public.
166. Will not scratch or adjust himself (by which I mean his man-parts) in public.
167. Will have a nice voice, deep and gentle.
168. Will speak at least two languages.
169. Will know how to behave in restaurants.
170. Will not start fights with people.
171. Will be strong enough that should a fight arise he will be able to finish it.
172. Will know about plumbing.
173. Will know about gardening.
174. Will not expect me to learn about, or be interested in, plumbing or gardening.
175. Will not undermine me.
176. If I gain weight, will still stay with me.
177. Will not become fat.
178. Will not lose his hair.
179. Will be decisive.
180. Will not boss me around.
181. Will be honest with me about clothing that does or does not suit me.
182. Will think I look lovely, no matter what I wear.
183. Will want to have my babies a little bit, even though I won't want his.

184. Will have a lithe, muscular frame like a sexy vampire who goes back to secondary school in order to find his soul-mate.

185. Will consider me his soul-mate.

186. Will complete me.

187. Will have a car when we are a bit older.

188. Will give me lifts to things, even if he isn't going to those things himself.

189. Will be quite deep, but not in a way that makes me feel shallow or stupid.

190. Will require my input for every important decision he makes.

191. Will be his own man.

192. Will be the strong silent type.

193. Will not be too quiet.

194. Will never have a goatee.

195. Will never have a tongue piercing.

196. Will never have a nipple or downstairs piercing.

197. Will never have a nose piercing.

198. Will not have a tattoo, unless it is a really beautiful one.

199. Will have enough confidence to model my man-hats in pictures for my portfolio.

200. Will not be a transvestite.

201. Will be the type of man who can pull off nail varnish and eyeliner.

202. Will not be the type of man who wears nail varnish and eyeliner all the time, though.

203. Will sit with me at parties when I am in one of my afraid-of-people moods.

204. Will look damn good in a tuxedo.

205. Will never drink and drive.

206. Will never, ever wear just a T-shirt and nothing else, like a freak.

207. Will sometimes wear well-fitting boxers and nothing else, like a man in a coffee ad.

208. Will be able to brew good coffee.

209. Will have jobs in cool shops and bars while we are in college.

210. Will accept that I am moving to London to be a milliner, so our relationship will have to be either long distance or over unless he moves with me.

211. Will be accepting of all different types of people and their beliefs.

212. Will not make fun of old women.

213. Will not talk down to me.

214. Will know stuff about cars.

215. Will be good at lifting things.

216. Will not lift things to excess, like a gross veiny body-builder.

217. Will have friends that gel well with my friends.

218. Will not have too many ex-girlfriends.

219. Will probably have to have some ex-girlfriends, though, because it adds an aura of desirability.

220. Will not wear an excess of hair product.

221. Will be open to a lot of gentle guidance as to what sort of clothing does and does not suit him.

222. Will enjoy listening to me sing as I go about the house doing bits and pieces.

223. Will not make fun of people to make himself feel more normal.

224. Will appreciate that we are all a little odd and that this is a beautiful thing.

225. Will have basic first-aid skills.

226. Will be confident and broad-shouldered.

227. Will not resemble a confident, broad-shouldered politician but rather a hot actor or musician or something.

228. Will think that I have 'fine eyes'.

229. Will watch soap operas with me and listen patiently as I explain the inter-connectedness of the characters' lives, and by extension humanity itself.

230. Will not tell Prim about the *High School Musical* watching that will probably happen.

231. Will take charge of a situation if needs be, but not in a bossy way.

232. Will never grow a beard with no moustache because that is creepy.

233. Will change his clothing and socks on an extremely regular basis.

234. Will be somebody I am in love with.

HELLO, this is the portion of the book where I get to talk to you directly for the purposes of thanking. Thanks to all the people who read and liked the first two, particularly the artist who managed to sneak a letter into my mum's handbag at my book launch. It makes me shine with happiness when people like Prim.

Someone who has always liked Prim is the wonderful Siobhán Parkinson, lady-boss of Islands and of words. I'm very grateful Siobhán, thanks a million.

At Siobhán's side, there used to be the magnificent Elaina O'Neill, but then she got another job and another name. Elaina Ryan, in the words of a hatless bear, 'Thank you anyway' for supportiveness and prim-thusiasm.

Gráinne Clear, thank you for helping this book be a book, I'm happy you get to work on the Little Island now. You're my prez always.

Fidelma Slattery, a woman of many talents who makes Prim's venting easy on the eye in an artful and creative manner.

Diarmuid O'Brien. You are my favourite human being. Thanks for listening and being there and having shoulders. 'No one is' is a lie.

Thanks...

Mary and Tim Sullivan, ye raised me. Well done there. Thanks for teaching me kindness and strength by example. I'll keep learning.

Alacoque Sullivan, dancer, artist and seasoned traveller. I love you, Nana.

Writing buddies make the world a better place: Sarah Maria Griffin and Dave Rudden, ye are the bosses of everything. I like working in COMPLETE SILENCE with ye.

Graham Tugwell, Claire Hennessy and Sheena Wilkinson for being marvellous at vent-listening and plot hashing.

To Ciara Banks and Suzanne Keaveney for being crazy supportive and marvellous.

To Donnacha O'Brien, for the shelves and promotional work. Go Go Team Danger!!

To Sinéad O'Brien for being a magnificent player and all round good friend.

And finally, to Joshua for teaching me that words do not equal communication, nor should they. To Neil for having fantastic taste in music and constantly trying his best, even when the world is very noisy. To Emma, who is great at writing letters and being kind to small and fragile things. To Josh, who taught me that everything is better if you are also singing. To Grace, for making old words new with her beautiful voice. And to Daniel for lighting up the room.